The Tainted Course
A Sugarbury Falls Mystery

by

Diane Weiner

For information, email Cozy Cat Press, cozycatpress@aol.com or visit our website at: www.cozycatpress.com

COZY CAT
PRESS

ISBN: 978-1-946063-81-6
Printed in the United States of America

10 9 8 7 6 5 4 3 2 1

This book is dedicated to my husband, Robert. His patience and ever present support are so greatly appreciated.

Chapter 1

Henry Fox pulled into the gravel lot in front of The Outside Inn. Although it was still winter, the unseasonably warm day had begun to melt the snow into dirty slush. "Watch out when you get out, Maddy. Don't step in the puddle." He walked around and opened the door for his wife, Emily. They'd been married going on thirty years and he still held doors open for her. One of the things she loved about him.

"I'm starving. I hope Coralee has her mac and cheese casserole on the menu tonight." Emily loosened her scarf. "What are you getting, Maddy?" No answer. "Maddy?"

Maddy pulled one of her air pods out of her ear. "What'd you say?"

"I said what are you in the mood to eat tonight?" She hated that Maddy couldn't be in the car for five minutes without needing to have the air pods in. She knew it was personal. Maybe the music wasn't even turned on. She suspected it was Maddy's way of avoiding conversation.

"Oh!" Maddy wiped off the bottom of her jeans. "Why didn't you tell me you'd parked in a puddle, Dad?"

"I did. Never mind." They climbed the porch steps and Henry held the door for both his ladies. Coralee Saunders, the owner, greeted them as usual with a big dose of hospitality.

"Maddy, Harriett was adopted this afternoon. Mrs. Blag finally gave into her daughter. Poor girl had been dragging her mom into the cat café every time they stopped by. Guess she succumbed to the pressure, though she herself cuddled that orange tabby like it was a baby. Now there are only four cats in the café. I think that's about the least we've had since you opened it."

Maddy, wringing the melted snow from the hem of her distressed jeans, looked up. "That's great. Another month and it'll be kitten season so it's good we'll have plenty of room."

Coralee grabbed three menus. "I tried a new vegetarian recipe tonight. Israeli couscous with grilled Roma tomatoes."

Coralee continually surprised Emily and Maddy with her enthusiasm for coming up with innovative vegetarian recipes for them, even though Coralee's favorite dish was a bacon cheeseburger, heavy on the bacon.

"Maddy, isn't that your friend Ava and her mother?" asked Emily.

A heavy set woman with short red hair sat between a teenager and a little girl.

"Yeah, it is." She walked over to her friend. "I missed you at school today."

"Mila had another seizure. I helped Mom get her to the emergency room. Believe me, I'd have rather been sitting through Geometry than waiting in a boring room with no internet service."

Emily said, "Sorry to hear that. Is she okay?" She couldn't remember Ava's mother's name. Embarrassing, since she normally had a reporter's mind for details.

"Poor baby has had random seizures since she was two. Thankfully, they're over quickly, but I always get her checked out just in case." She extended her hand to

Henry. "Faith Maguire. I've seen you at the hospital, but we haven't formally met."

"Henry Fox. How are you enjoying being the new school superintendent?"

"It's only been, what, six months, but so far so good. I don't miss my old commute; I can tell you that. Atlanta traffic is crazy bad at any hour. I've yet to find traffic in Vermont. And Ava and Milo can attend the local schools here. Back home, the local high school was so bad Ava stayed with her Dad during the school year."

The waitress brought over drinks. "Are you ready to order?"

"Would the three of you like to join us for dinner?" said Faith.

Emily looked at Henry, who looked at Maddy for a clue as to how to answer.

Maddy said, "Sure."

"Miss," said Faith, "Can you grab three more chairs for our friends?"

"Your wish is my command." When the waitress turned to grab the chairs, the tray knocked into Faith Maguire's glass, spilling Diet Coke all over the white tablecloth and worse, all over Faith's white pants.

"Can't you be more careful? Where do they find the help these days?"

The waitress said, "Oh, I don't know. Maybe Coralee finds Harmon College students who were cheated out of an education thanks to a nosy, old..."

Coralee stepped in. "Summer, that's enough now. Take a break and then swap tables with Lou Ellen." Coralee patted the spilled soda with a clean towel. "Come, move over here." She led them to a new table by the window, overlooking the snow-covered golf course. "I'll send Lou Ellen right over." She left Faith a clean napkin with which to blot her pants.

Maddy said, "I think she knocked over the drinks on purpose. What was that about?"

Faith said, "Nothing. I'm sure it was an accident. Now, what's good here? We were here for brunch once, but never for dinner."

Emily said, "Maddy and I don't eat meat, but the mac and cheese is great and so is the linguine primavera. I don't know how Coralee manages to find fresh vegetables in the middle of winter in Vermont but she does."

"I want mac and cheese," said Mila.

"Honey, you know you can't have dairy, it might cause another seizure. How about a burger?"

Mila said, "Okay, Mommy." She folded her hands, looking disappointed.

Not having gone through the early stages of parenthood, Emily was surprised that Mila didn't put up a fuss. "What grade are you in, Mila?"

"Second. I'm in Miss Pratt's class."

Maddy perked up. "Miss Pratt? She's my half-sister! Do you like her?"

"She's the best. She says I have the best handwriting in the class. And when I don't feel good, she lets me put my head down."

"What a coincidence," said Faith. "Miss Pratt says she's new in town also."

"Yes. She graduated with her teaching degree last spring and then she found out I was her half-sister so she came to visit. Then she saw a job posting and applied for the teaching position."

"Fortunate for us," said Faith. "It's hard finding good teachers these days."

"Maybe if they paid them better or respected them more...don't get me started," said Emily.

"I couldn't agree with you more. I'm hoping to attract new talent to our district."

Lou Ellen came to the table to take their orders. Everyone took Emily's suggestion and ordered the mac and cheese. Faith ordered a burger for Mila.

Henry said, "Ava, where does your dad live? It must be an adjustment not seeing him every day."

"I really miss him. He lives in Savannah, Georgia. Mom won't let me see him at all anymore."

"Now, don't put it like that, Ava."

"You know it's true. You got the court to take away his visitation rights. I can't believe you could be so cruel. Mila won't even remember him by the time she grows up."

"Stop being a drama queen, Ava. And stop airing our dirty laundry in front of strangers, um, new friends."

"He hates you, you know. He said he wished you'd drop dead."

The silence hung over the table like still air on a humid day. Emily wished the food would come so she could at least have something to focus on.

"Ava, do you and Maddy have all the same classes?" Henry took a sip of water.

"Mostly. I'm taking painting as an elective though."

"Painting, huh? I make furniture as a hobby. I could throw a bookshelf your way if you want practice."

Ava smiled, tension diffused by Henry's talent for peace making.

"And you know I'm in band," said Maddy. "You can't be in both."

"Hey, Maddy. I'll bet painting wouldn't make Chester flee the room like when you practice."

"Thanks, Dad. You're so supportive."

Lou Ellen, thankfully, returned quickly with the food.

"Delicious," said Faith. "How's your burger, Mila?"

"Good, but I'm not that hungry."

Henry said, "I'll bet when you see the desserts Coralee makes you'll be plenty hungry."

Faith glared at him. "I rarely let her have sugar."

"Really? I'm a physician and I say a little dessert now and then is good for you."

Emily cleared her throat. Faith's phone vibrated on the table. "Hello? Yes, Tilly. That's fine. We're eating dinner at the Outside Inn. We'll be home in a little while." She put down the phone. "That was our housekeeper/nurse. She spent the day in Burlington and wanted to let me know she was back."

A handsome Hispanic man followed Coralee through the dining room.

"Arturo, it's the bulb over there by the window."

Arturo stopped in his tracks when he spotted Faith. "You! What are you doing here? You're the one who should have been banned from the country, you old witch." He grabbed a chair as if he was about to use it to hit Faith. Coralee stopped him.

"Arturo, what's the matter with you? This woman is a guest. You can't work here and treat people like that. I'm afraid..."

"Don't fire him, I'm sure this is the best paying job he can find since there aren't apples to pick in the winter time." Faith took a sip of her tea.

Arturo grabbed for the chair again. Coralee grabbed his wrist. "Calm down. You can change the bulb later, it's not that important."

Arturo shook his finger in Faith's face. "You cost my sister her job and now she's back in Mexico all alone while her family is here."

"That's what happens when you sneak into this country. Don't try to tell me she didn't know any better."

"Arturo, let's go." Coralee's voice was stern. She apologized to the table and led Arturo out of the dining room.

Henry said, "Maybe we should be going."

"No, he's not going to ruin our evening. You mentioned dessert earlier. Waitress!" Faith signaled for Lou Ellen to come over. "We'd like to see a dessert menu."

"I can tell you the special desserts tonight. We have cheesecake, Boston cream pie, and apple strudel with vanilla ice cream."

"I'm stuffed," said Emily. She seldom turned down dessert, no matter how full she was, but she'd had enough of this anything but relaxing dinner.

Henry said, "We can get dessert to go, how's that? Save it for when we've had time to digest our meal. Coralee's desserts aren't something to pass up."

Emily knew Henry couldn't pass up the apple strudel. "Fine. Two apple strudels. We have ice cream at home in the freezer. What would you like, Maddy? Same as Dad?"

"Yeah."

When the desserts were ready to go, Ava said, "I'll see you at school tomorrow." She looked at her mother. "Right, Mom?"

"Of course. I only needed you to help me today because Tilly had the day off. Henry and Emily, it's been a pleasure. Maddy, I'm sure we'll see you soon."

Chapter 2

The next morning, Emily knocked on Maddy's door. "Time to get up. Dad made waffles. If you hurry, you'll have time to eat them before school." She went into the kitchen and poured food into Chester's bowl. Henry sat at the counter reading the newspaper while monitoring the waffle iron.

"What an experience last night. Ava's mother has been in town what, six months? In the course of an hour's dinner we met two people who hate her," said Henry. "When Maddy came to live with us, remember how worried we were about being good parents to a teenager? After having dinner with Faith Maguire, I'd say Maddy is lucky to have us. I think Fiona is up there in heaven smiling that she chose the right guardian."

"What brought that on? Do you hear it?"

"Hear what?"

"Harp music coming from the sky."

"Very funny. I don't know. I think we set a good example for Maddy to follow. I saw how Faith was with the first waitress and the handyman. She talked down to them and obviously had hurt them. And look how her little daughter was afraid of her."

"Afraid?"

"As soon as Mommy said no dairy the poor kid pulled back. She never said she wanted a burger and did you notice she hardly ate two bites?"

"I guess Faith was trying to do what was best for her health. I can't imagine having a child with seizures. Must be difficult."

"Show me a piece of literature that ties seizures in with eating dairy."

Maddy came into the kitchen. "I heard you made waffles."

"Sorry, the early worm gets the bird. Or is it the early…"

Emily pointed to a platter full of waffles. "Stop teasing her, Henry. She's already running late for school. Maddy, does that skirt meet the dress code? It's a little short."

"I'm wearing tights and boots so stop tripping. I wore it last week and you didn't say anything." She grabbed a paper plate and made herself a waffle to go. "I have to catch the bus."

As usual, Emily heard the door slam. "Didn't you think that skirt was too short? I don't want to get called down to the school to pick her up because she doesn't meet the dress code. Maddy certainly isn't afraid of me, that's for sure. Sometimes I'm a little afraid of her with that teenage temper."

Henry hugged her. "Stop tripping, Mama. You've got to pick your battles. Hey, want some strudel to go with those waffles?" He opened the fridge and took out two Styrofoam containers.

"Dessert first thing in the morning?"

"Of course not. Second thing in the morning. I had waffles first." He dipped forkfuls of strudel into the leftover syrup on his plate. "I've got the early shift at the hospital. I'll be home before dinner."

"I'll be at St. Edwards. Class ends at 3:00. Then I have office hours. I'll take my dessert with me."

Henry drove to the community hospital. He'd retired before moving to Vermont when he was barely old enough to join the AARP and realizing the need for medical care in Sugarbury Falls, opted to work part time at the hospital. He ran into his buddy, Pat in the parking lot.

"You look like you slept in your clothes."

"Funny. I was over at Megan's watching Netflix and I fell asleep. My patients don't complain about how I look."

"Seeing as they're dead, I guess not. Things are going well with Megan, aren't they?"

"Very. After Carol died, I imagined a lonely life ahead of me. Megan changed all that."

"Your very own detective to watch out for you. When are you going to put a ring on it?"

"As a matter of fact, I'm planning to. Just trying to pick the right time and place. Ring's in my dresser drawer waiting."

"Congrats, buddy. Megan is a prize. Do you think she'll say yes?"

Pat nodded his head. "And to think I was going to ask you to be my best man."

An ambulance sped by as they neared the hospital entrance.

"Looks like the day's starting off with a bang. Catch you later," said Henry.

Henry had no sooner put on his white coat when he was pulled into Emergency. The paramedics were frantically trying to revive a lifeless woman. Henry took over compressions. He sensed she was already gone, but gave it his best effort. "Paddles. Clear. Try again. Clear. Epi…" No response.

"It's too late. Time of death, 8:43 am." He pulled the curtain closed and turned to the paramedics. "What happened?"

"The housekeeper called 911. She found the patient collapsed on the bedroom floor. She figured it was a heart attack."

A short, middle-aged woman ran into the ER. "Is she okay? Where's Faith?"

Faith? Henry put it together. Oh, my God, the woman on the table was Ava's mother, Faith Maguire. The one they'd eaten dinner with last night. He'd been so busy trying to save her, he hadn't noticed. He took a deep breath so he'd have a shot at sounding professional. "Are you the next of kin?"

"I'm the housekeeper/nanny. Me and her daughters are her family. I'm Tilly Armstrong."

He cleared his throat. "I'm sorry to tell you this, but Ms. Maguire didn't pull through."

"What do you mean? I...when I saw her last night she was perfectly fine. Alive. I tucked in Mila and she was helping Ava with her homework. This morning, I got the girls off to school and she, and she still wasn't awake. I...I found her collapsed on the floor by the bed and called 911. What am I going to tell the girls?"

Henry said, "Is there someone we can call?"

"What about the girls? They're in school. Should I pick them up?"

"How about the girls' father? They're divorced, right?"

"Yes. I should, I can...I'll call him but he's in Georgia."

"Call him. Maybe he should be the one to tell them."

"What should I say? Was it a heart attack?"

"I'll let you know as soon as we can determine the cause of death. Did she have a heart condition, allergies, or any other medical condition you know of?"

"No heart problems or allergies that I know of. I've only worked for her the past few months. She has type two diabetes. Do you think that's what killed her?"

"Without examining her, I can't say. We'll be in contact as soon as we know something."

After Tilly Armstrong left the hospital, Henry called Pat in the morgue. "Do you have time to look at a recently deceased patient? She's the mother of Maddy's friend."

"I'll squeeze her in. Give me a couple of hours."

"Thanks, Pat." Always protective of his new daughter, he worried about how the news would affect Maddy. Maddy had lost her own mother, which is how she came to be their daughter. On the one hand, she'd be a comfort to Ava. After all, she'd recently been through it. On the other, the wound was still recent. Some nights he heard Maddy crying into her pillow when he passed by her room to say good night. Emily would know how to handle this. He gave her a call and relayed the details.

Emily said, "That's awful. How did she die? We just had dinner with her last night."

"Most likely a heart attack. Pat's taking a look. The housekeeper is going to call the father. We have to tell Maddy right after school before she hears it from elsewhere."

"Okay, I'll cut my office hours short. Let me know what Pat finds out."

"Em, what if this sets Maddy back? It's been a long road, her coping with Fiona's death."

"She's resilient. She'll be okay. In fact, she's in the best position to help Ava through this."

Not fully convinced, but wanting to believe his wife, he said, "You're probably right. Gotta go, love you."

Henry kept busy with patients all morning. Just before lunch, Pat called.

"Hey, Buddy. I've got some news about your patient."

"Heart attack?"

"Nope. Her blood sugar crashed."

"What? Too much insulin?"

"She wasn't on insulin, just oral diabetes medication."

"An accidental overdose?"

"Not with the amount she had in her system. It had to be intentional."

"Intentional? You mean…"

"I mean if it wasn't suicide, it was murder."

Chapter 3

Emily received a frantic call from Coralee just as her class ended. "What do you mean shutting down the inn? Who's shutting it down?"

"The police are here. They have a warrant and they're searching my kitchen. Throwing boxes of food out of the pantry, pouring samples of milk from the fridge…" She told Emily to hold on while she yelled at the police. "Careful, that's my Grandmother's mixing bowl!"

"Coralee, you still there?"

"I'm here. I…I can't breathe."

"Go out of the kitchen. Slow down. In through the nose, out through the mouth. Tell me what's going on."

"You know that woman who you had dinner with last night?"

"Faith Maguire. Henry told me the housekeeper found her this morning. He thinks it was a heart attack."

"No heart attack. A drug overdose. And guess where they think she got the drug?"

"Drug? What drug? Where?"

"They found traces of it in the cheesecake she brought home with her. The cheesecake from my kitchen!"

"That's impossible. Did anyone else get sick?"

"Not that I know of. I feel terrible. What if I was somehow responsible? And when word gets out, no one will want to stay here."

"Look, I'll contact my teaching assistant to cover my class and I'll be right over."

Emily felt sick. Faith Maguire, not only dead, but apparently murdered. Unless, of course, she accidentally ate poison cheesecake. Right. How long after she ate it did she...? Was it only the cheesecake or other desserts as well? Emily reassured herself. It'd been hours since they'd eaten the strudel. Surely if they were going to die they'd be dead by now, right? She called Henry from the car.

"Henry, Coralee just called and..."

"The cheesecake killed Faith Maguire. I know. Pat thinks it had been laced with a diabetes drug."

"Insulin?"

"No, an oral diabetes medication. It caused her blood sugar to drop too low which resulted in her death."

"We ate there, too. Do we need to seek treatment?" She had a horrible thought. "And what about Maddy!"

"Maddy hasn't eaten hers, it's still in the fridge. We'd be dead by now if we'd ingested it. And no one has come through the emergency department with suspicious symptoms. The housekeeper said Faith Maguire was taking diabetes meds."

"Could she have simply taken too much of the drug herself?"

"The dose had to have been massive. Megan and Detective Ron are searching the kitchen at the inn."

"I know. Poor Coralee is in a panic. I'm headed there now. Hopefully it will be resolved by the time I get there."

"Hold on. It's going to take a while to test everything in that kitchen. The medication could have been in any of the ingredients used to make the cake, or added after the cake was made."

"What about Ava and Mila? The poor girls! Do they know?"

"Not yet, they're at school. Tilly, the housekeeper, is contacting their father. He should be able to get here by this evening if not sooner."

"Okay. I'm pulling up to the inn now. I'll talk to you later."

The sight of the police cars in front of the inn made her nauseous. Coralee was the kindest person she knew and the idea that something from her kitchen killed someone would crush her.

Detective Megan O'Leary was Pat the pathologist's girlfriend. She and her partner, Ron Wooster, stood guard at the entrance to the inn. A dozen or so guests shivered outside on the porch, too curious to go back to the comfort of their rooms.

"Megan, can I go in? Coralee called and told me what happened."

"As long as you stay out of the kitchen. Coralee is in the lobby."

"You know she isn't responsible for this."

Detective Ron said, "Of course, she didn't do it intentionally, but someone poisoned that cheesecake and it came from her kitchen."

"So it's a matter of who had access, right?"

"Yes, and the list is long. Members of the wait staff, kitchen help, even a guest could have slipped into the kitchen."

She turned to Megan. "You don't think the killer targeted Faith Maguire, do you?"

"So far, no one else who ate the cheesecake was affected. Of course, there are sickos who do this sort of thing randomly. Remember the Tylenol scare back a decade or so ago?"

"Or it could be someone who wanted to see the inn shut down," offered Ron.

Megan said, "Did Coralee have any enemies? It's hard to imagine."

"No, but Ron may be on to something. A new bed and breakfast opened up just a short time ago. I'm sure having the Outside Inn out of the picture would help their business." Could someone with the desire to run a bed and breakfast be capable of murder? Not the norm, but in her true crime writing, she'd been surprised more than once.

Coralee came to the door and fell into Emily's arms, sobbing. "I can't believe this is happening. What if they arrest me?"

Detective Megan said, "Coralee, this wasn't your fault. It's not like you were negligent and had a dining room full of deaths. This was done by an outsider with an axe to grind, or a psycho with his own agenda."

An axe to grind...Emily said, "Last night, two different people seemed to have had that axe to grind. Remember the Hispanic guy who said something about his sister?"

"Arturo. His sister worked for Faith Maguire when Faith and the girls first moved to town. Faith found out she was illegal and had her deported back to Mexico."

Megan scribbled down the info. "Arturo?"

"Arturo Rivera. His sister's name is Maria Luz."

Emily said, "And what about the one who made the comment about not getting into Harmon College? The waitress. I think she deliberately spilled Diet Coke in Faith's lap. I felt the tension in her voice."

Coralee said, "That's Summer Martin. She was supposed to start college last fall but something happened. I'm not one to gossip, so I'll leave it at that. Summer came to me begging for a job last fall."

Emily said, "There's our first two suspects. Both had access to the kitchen last night and both had motive. Both were unpleasantly surprised to see Faith Maguire at the inn and made no attempt to hide it."

"I can't believe either of them would do something like this. Maybe it was someone associated with the new inn."

Megan took notes. Detective Wooster and I will get on it. Coralee, can you make a list of who was here last night? Employees with their contact information, and you must have a list of all the guests who are staying here."

Emily added, "Some of the diners weren't guests, though. Shouldn't we look into them, too?"

"Detective Wooster and I will check the credit card records and Coralee, do you have a list of reservations?"

"Yes, but we always manage to seat walk-ins as well. And though rare, some actually pay with cash."

"We have enough to start with. Meanwhile, the guests will have to eat elsewhere for now." Megan left, telling the guests they could go inside but not into the kitchen or dining areas.

Coralee paced in front of the front desk. "That's all I need. Where do you think my guests are going to eat? They'll be headed right to the new inn, you'll see."

"There are plenty of restaurants downtown. I'll help you compile a list."

"And none are as close as Smyth Haven. What a disaster. Even if police find nothing, you know how people talk. It'll take months for this to blow over."

"I have to pick up something I forgot in my office, but on my way back from St. Edwards, I'll stop at some local restaurants and see if they're willing to offer coupons or special deals for your guests."

"Emily, I can always count on you." She hugged Emily goodbye.

Emily wished she could simply go back home and work on her current true crime book, but she promised her students she'd have the first drafts of their book synopses back to them by tomorrow. If only she'd taken a minute to throw them into her bag before she rushed over to the inn...Maddy was at school, and Henry at the hospital. It would have been a good time to get some writing done.

St. Edwards was a small liberal arts college nestled between pine trees at the outskirt of town. Emily's office building looked like a stone castle straight out of a fairy tale. She pulled into the lot and walked to her office.

"Knock, knock. I didn't expect to see you back here today. I thought your TA was taking your afternoon class."

"Come on in, Nance. Yes, but I forgot the assignments I promised the students I'd grade." She picked up a stack from her desk. "It's going to be a long night."

"Then let's get coffee to get you started." Nancy was Emily's colleague and had become a close friend. She had a daughter Maddy's age and when Emily found herself guardian to her deceased college roommate's teen daughter, she wouldn't have made it in one piece if not for Nancy's advice and support.

"Sure." She zipped her jacket and they followed the cobblestone path toward the student union. "You heard about the murder last night, right?"

"I heard it on the car radio. Murder? They were referring to it as a suspicious death."

"We ate dinner with the victim and her daughters last night at Coralee's. We all ordered dessert; it could have been us just as easily as it was Faith."

"I'm so sorry. I didn't realize you knew the victim."

"We just met last night. Maddy's friends with Ava, her daughter."

"Ava Maguire? I didn't put it together. Brooke and Ava are classmates, too. They went to the mall just last weekend. I dropped them off. Who would do such a thing?"

"Two of Coralee's staff had motive. Both were there last night. One was a handyman named Arturo Rivera. The other was a waitress."

"What motives did they have?"

"Arturo Rivera claims Faith Maguire had his sister deported back to Mexico. Summer made a comment about not being able to go to her dream college."

"Are you talking about Summer Martin?"

"I didn't get her last name. Why?"

"Don't you remember? It was all over the news."

"What was?"

"Summer Martin is the District Attorney's daughter. Margaret Martin bribed the president of Harmon College to accept Summer for admission to this year's freshman class."

"I saw a story about it on the news. She wasn't the only one involved. Wasn't that Broadway actor accused of doing the same for his kid?"

"Yes, and a handful of other influential types. Shameful. If she mentioned Harmon College, it has to be Summer Martin."

"So you think Faith Maguire is responsible for getting her thrown out?"

"She tipped off the press. It was right before the semester started. Summer had already moved into her dorm and everything."

"We were in Scotland most of the summer so I didn't get all the details."

"Margaret Martin was disbarred and Summer was humiliated. I see motive there."

"She was right there in the dining room. Surely she could have spiked Faith's dessert.

I'll have to tell Megan."

Emily checked her watch. "Got to go. Henry and I want to break the news to Maddy before she hears it elsewhere."

When she got home, Henry was waiting in the living room.

"Is Maddy home yet?"

"She's in her room."

"Are you ready to break the news to her?"

"Break the news? It was all over social media according to Maddy. By lunch the whole school knew."

"How did she take it?"

"She's upset, of course. She's worried about Ava. The housekeeper picked the girls up early from school and Maddy's been trying to text Ava but she's not answering."

"She expected Ava to be on her phone at a time like this? Their father was supposed to arrive tonight, right?"

"Yeah, but there's a big snow storm in the Southeast. The flights are likely to be delayed or even canceled, especially if he's going through Atlanta. They're getting the worst of it."

"I'll go check on Maddy."

"Honestly, I think she needs her space right now. She was in no mood to talk. Let's wait until morning."

Chapter 4

The next morning, Emily collected her thoughts while she microwaved a bowl of oatmeal. Henry had already left for the hospital. She fed Chester, rinsed the breakfast dishes, poured another cup of coffee, then knocked on Maddy's door. Enough procrastinating. She had to talk to Maddy before she left.

"Honey, are you okay? Can I come in?" She half expected her to grumble and tell her to go away.

"Come in."

Maddy's eyes were red and Emily saw the bedside picture of Fiona, Maddy's mother, on the pillow. "This must be hard for you."

"I can't stop thinking about Ava and her sister. I know how it feels to lose your mother. I wish she'd answer my calls or at least text back."

"I can't imagine how torn up she must be. I'm glad her father came. Why don't you just send her a text saying you know what she's going through and if she wants to talk, you're there whenever she's ready."

"I pretty much said that. Did Dad leave already?"

"Yes. I'm heading to Coralee's. Do you want me to drop you off at school?"

"No, the bus will be here in a few minutes." Emily followed her into the kitchen. Maddy put her cereal bowl in the sink and grabbed her backpack. She started to leave and then turned around and gave Emily a hug. "I miss my mother every day, but I was lucky to wind up with you and Dad."

Emily's heart felt as though it was crying. So many times she wondered if Maddy even liked her let alone appreciated her. "Bye, honey. I love you." She wiped her own tears.

After Maddy left, Emily stopped by the inn to check on Coralee. The parking lot in front of the inn was eerily quiet. She got the chills when she went inside and saw the yellow crime scene tape across the dining room entrance.

"Emily, thanks for coming over." Coralee's eyes were red and her hair looked as though it hadn't been brushed. Emily rarely saw Coralee with so much as a wrinkle in her clothing or an untucked tendril. She gave her a hug.

"How are you holding up?"

"I've been better. This is all my fault. Thank God no one else has gotten ill—as least not yet."

"Coralee, it's not your fault."

"Then whose fault is it? I'm responsible for who and what gets in my kitchen. If the ingredients were tainted, or someone snuck in..."

"Let's try to figure this out. If the ingredients were bad, more people would be ill or dead right now."

It took Coralee a minute, then she answered, "I suppose you're right."

"We have to think. If this was intentional, who had motive and opportunity?"

"Any of my staff, the delivery man...I suppose a guest could walk in unnoticed during a busy period."

"How long has Summer Martin worked for you?"

"Summer? I hired her last fall. I'm not one to gossip, but the poor girl was yanked out of college thanks to her crooked mother."

"I heard."

"Some district attorney bribing her daughter's way into college. Summer didn't know. Poor girl came looking for a job, hoping to take some classes at St. Edwards next semester after things have a chance to blow over. She's been nothing but reliable."

"She was pretty rude last night at dinner."

"Do you blame her? Faith Maguire changed the course of the poor girl's life. A degree from Harmon College opens all kinds of doors. It's like the Harvard of the east."

"Harvard is in the east, but I get your point. Do you know if she had access to a diabetes drug? Not insulin, an oral medication."

"I wouldn't be surprised if one of our guests takes it. I do. So do half the overweight people in this town."

"That's because they flock to your desserts. I've gained ten pounds since I discovered your cheesecake and apple strudel." Why did she say cheesecake? She should have left it at strudel. Emily cringed at her own lack of sensitivity.

"Not any more they won't. It'll take time before people trust my cooking again."

"Does Summer have access to the guest rooms?"

"No. Well, not regularly. She cleans rooms for me on occasion when the regular maid takes time off."

"Did that happen recently?"

"Yes. Yesterday as a matter of fact."

"Can we find out if any of the guests take that medication or are missing some?"

"How? Asking is an invasion of privacy, don't you think?"

Emily tried to come up with a plan. "Maybe you can say there have been thefts and you are asking if anything's gone missing."

"Oh, great. First a murder, then burglaries. I'll be out of business in a heartbeat."

Emily figured guests wouldn't bat an eye over burglary after hearing about a potential murder, but she put herself in Coralee's shoes. There had to be a way to find out if Summer Martin had access to the drug. Summer seemed genuinely surprised to see Faith at the inn last night. She would have had to swipe the medication during the dinner window.

"Summer doesn't have diabetes, does she?"

"Not that I know of. She eats a lot of salads and she is far from overweight."

"It's still possible, though unlikely." She'd ask Henry if he could find out through his hospital contacts. On second thought, he'd say it was unethical.

"Coralee, do you know which guests were eating in the dining room last night and which ones stayed in their rooms?"

"I've got a list of reservations, but I'm not the only restaurant in town. Just because someone didn't eat in my dining room, it doesn't mean they stayed in their room."

"Keep your eyes and ears open. Does Summer live here at the inn?"

"Yes. She gets the employee discount rate. Can't find cheaper rent in this town."

"And what about Arturo? Does he live here too?"

"Yeah. He was living with his sister before she was deported. Moved out of his cabin after he spent every cent he had trying to keep his sister in the country."

"How come his sister was deported but not him?"

"He was born here, she wasn't. She came on a student visa and just never went back home."

"Could he have spiked Faith's cheesecake?"

"I don't know. He was here but I can't see him as a murderer. When he isn't busy, he goes into the cat café and talks to the cats. They love him."

An elderly couple rang the front desk bell. "New guests? Emily, I've got to go."

"See, not everyone is scared away. I've got to head to class." She kissed her on the cheek. "It's going to be okay."

Emily headed to work. On the way, she passed a sign for the new bed and breakfast. Perhaps some coffee to go would be a good idea. She checked her watch. She had a few minutes to spare.

Smyth Haven was a renovated farm house. When the elderly owners died, their daughter inherited it and turned it into an inn. It had just opened last fall and was now catering to skiers. The parking lot wasn't huge, but it was full. Coralee had vacancies even before last night which was unusual at this time of year. Emily walked into the lobby.

"I'm sorry, we have no rooms available right now. I could get you in the end of March."

"Hi, I'm not actually here about a room. I was wondering if I could get two cups of coffee to-go? And some sort of muffins or donuts." She extended her hand. "Emily Fox. I teach at St. Edwards College."

"Rona Smyth. Emily Fox? There's an author named Emily Fox. I love her true crime books."

"That would be me."

"I'm honored to meet you," said the fortyish woman with the butterfly tattoo on her wrist. She wiped her hands on her apron before shaking Emily's hand. Her clothing smelled of smoke and irritated Emily's throat. "The dining room is closed until lunch, but we always have fresh coffee and sweets for the guests. I'll get you some."

Emily looked around. The lobby was papered with sepia toned trees and vintage horse drawn carriages on a cream colored background. Dull compared to Coralee's cheery lobby. The guest book was splayed open on the front counter. Brochures on the desk advertised Smyth Haven, the newest oldest inn in

Sugarbury Falls. She browsed at the prices. Wow, it was quite a bit cheaper to stay here than at the Outside Inn. She wondered if the food was nearly as good.

The owner emerged from around the corner carrying take-out coffee and a small white bag.

You have no idea how hard it is to resist the aroma of donuts. My doctor warned me about watching my sugar. If the guests didn't like them so much, I wouldn't torture myself."

"I've got a sweet tooth as well."

She handed Emily a brochure. "Do you live locally?"

"Yes. I teach part time at St. Edwards. I'm headed there now. Looks like your business is booming."

"We've been blessed. Had a rush this morning. Apparently there was a murder over at the competition."

"It wasn't a murder per say. No one died on the premises." If that didn't sound like a desperate defense...

"But the dessert came from their kitchen. Something like this happened where I used to live. Food poisoning, not even murder. Put the competition out of business."

"Have you been in the industry long?"

"Yes. Spent years working in hotels and restaurants. Always dreamed of having my own hotel one day. What a better tribute to my parents than to make my dream come true right in the house in which I grew up."

"Must have been tough drumming up business with the Outside Inn and the Ramada down the road."

"The Ramada Inn is a chain hotel, a totally different experience. The Outside Inn was our real competitor but we've managed to draw customers. With the bad press they're getting now, it won't be long until they're out of business."

Emily felt her blood boiling, but didn't want to tip her hand. "Do you work every night?"

"Of course. I'm the owner. Occasionally I get away for a few hours."

"Were you here last night? It was storming pretty bad later on. My poor cat wouldn't come out from under the bed."

"I'd been at a friend's place for dinner. Got in before the storm."

"Thanks for the coffee and treats. What do I owe you?"

"It's on the house. Take some brochures and spread them out around your office if you don't mind."

"Thank you, I will." On the way out, Emily noticed a pair of galoshes next to the umbrella stand. They were caked with red-brown dirt.

As soon as she got out the front door, Emily tossed the brochures in the trash. Undercutting Coralee? Did Megan and Ron check her alibi? If they hadn't yet, she was sure they would shortly. Was Rona Smyth really with a friend, or did she sneak into Coralee's kitchen and poison dessert to eliminate the competition?

Emily got back in the car, the aroma of fresh donuts tugging at her from the passenger seat. No, these were for her colleagues. Maybe just one…

As her hand reached into the bag, a call came over the Bluetooth. Her doctor's office? Why would they be calling?

"Hello, yes, this is Emily Fox."

"Mrs. Fox, we received the results of your mammogram. The breast center would like you to return for a more detailed follow-up and an ultrasound as soon as possible."

The words rattled between her ears. "Follow-up?" She'd been having routine mammograms for the past twenty years and was never asked to return. "Did they find cancer?" The C word stuck in her throat.

"They simply need a clearer view of one area. It happens more often than you'd think. Don't worry, just get it scheduled."

Emily jammed on her brakes, about to go through one of two traffic lights in the town. Breast cancer? She shook thinking about it. She was only fifty-five. Maybe this office had less sophisticated equipment than...than in the other small town she lived in before moving here? She'd had a mammogram here last year and it was fine. This year's technician seemed awfully tired. She'd even told her she'd been up all night with her new baby. She probably didn't set it up properly.

She pulled in behind her office at St. Edwards. She started to call Henry, then decided against it. She didn't want him to worry, and certainly didn't want anything to slip which would alarm Maddy. Maddy already lost her biological mother. The last thing she needed was to worry about losing her new mother, too.

Chapter 5

Henry put on his white coat and hit the ground running. His first patient was an elderly man experiencing abdominal pain. He went from there to a teen suffering an asthma attack. For a small town, the emergency room was disproportionately busy. The winter brought recreational snow enthusiasts who inevitably overdid it; the summer brought insect bites, broken bones, and heat related emergencies. Although he'd planned to retire early and live the life of leisure when they inherited his parents' cabin, he'd grown a bit bored rather quickly, and couldn't ignore how desperate the hospital was for help.

"Who's next?" asked Henry. The nurse pointed him toward a cubicle. He thought he recognized the man, but with the swollen nose and black eye, he wasn't certain.

"I think my nose is broke. I'm supposed to work this afternoon. Can you fix it by then?"

Henry looked at the paperwork. Arturo Rivera, age 29. He was at Coralee's last night and accused Faith of having his sister deported! "Tell me what happened." He put on his gloves and gently examined Arturo's nose.

"It was a bar fight."

"Looks like it was quite a fight."

"You should see the other guy."

Henry noticed him flinching when he attempted to laugh. "Does your chest hurt, too?"

"Yeah, when I cough or laugh…or move."

"We'll get some x-rays. A bar fight?"

"A gringo wearing a flag t-shirt called me amigo. I told him I was not his amigo. He did it again and I swung at him."

"Bar fights are rare in Sugarbury Falls. The nose looks broken, and I suspect you've got a few injured ribs as well. They'll take you to radiology and when the films come back, we'll see what we're dealing with."

"Gracias, doctor."

Shortly after noon, Pat stopped by.

"Ready for lunch, Buddy?"

"Yeah. Chez Cafeteria?"

"Cafeteria it is. I can smell the grease already."

"Just treated a guy who was in a bar fight."

"Ah, I was with Megan last night and she got an emergency call to Andy's bar. Apparently, it was pretty bad."

"The guy says it was racial. Someone called him amigo."

"So? Amigo means friend, right?"

"He said it in a derogatory way."

"Yeah, but according to Megan, he came in heated and took the first swing. Not saying the first guy didn't deserve it."

"It must have been after he finished at Coralee's. He was working last night."

"It was pretty late when Megan got the call. Speaking of Megan, I'm trying to plan the perfect proposal. Something a little unusual, but romantic."

"You mean like renting a billboard, or getting down on one knee at a Patriots game?"

"Yeah, but not so public. Her birthday is coming up."

"Take her away for the weekend and take her for a romantic dinner. You already have the ring."

"She doesn't have a full weekend off until after Easter."

"I'll ask Emily. She's creative."

"Only if she promises not to let the cat out of the bag. I want this to be a surprise."

"You got it." He grabbed a tray and picked up a veggie burger. His wife and daughter were beginning to rub off on him.

Pat took a cheeseburger and fries, then at the register, added a bag of M&Ms.

"Better cut back on the junk food if you want to look good in a tux."

"Megan says I look good in anything. Or nothing."

"TMI, buddy. Too much information."

Detective Megan and her partner, Ron Wooster, walked into the cafeteria. When they came to the table, Pat gave Megan a kiss on the cheek.

"What are you two doing here? The food isn't all that great."

Ron said, "We didn't come for the food. Henry, we know you treated a patient named Arturo Rivera this morning. We wanted to ask a few questions."

"I don't know what help I'll be, but shoot."

Ron said, "He was in a bar fight last night. The person he got into it with wants to press charges. He claims he barely pushed Arturo Rivera, then Arturo went postal on him. What are the extent of Rivera's wounds? Does it look as if the other guy fought back?"

"I'll say. Arturo Rivera was sent for imaging, but I'm almost positive he has a broken nose and at least one cracked rib."

"Then they share responsibility."

"Arturo said the man called him *amigo* and provoked him."

"Amigo? That's it?" Ron Wooster added the information on his iPad. "We tried to question him but he must have been getting his tests done. We'll go back up. Are you admitting him?"

"No, we'll fix him up best we can and send him home with painkillers. He's probably back in the ER by now."

"Thanks for the info. Say hi to Emily and Maddy."

"Will do."

Pat said, "Megan, I'll pick you up at seven."

"Looking forward to it." She followed her partner out of the cafeteria.

Henry took a sip of his coffee. "If Arturo Rivera has that quick of a trigger, I can't imagine him having the patience to steal the diabetes drug and spike Faith's dessert. I'd think he'd more likely run her over with a car or hit her over the head."

"You never know. If he was enraged by seeing the person who sent his sister out of the country, he may have gotten into a mode."

"Not to speak ill of the dead, but I imagine Faith Maguire rubbed many people the wrong way. I only met her once and took an instant dislike to her."

"You? You like everyone."

"That's what I mean."

"I'd better head back upstairs. Arturo's results should be back by now."

"We still on for Saturday night?"

"Of course."

"What time?"

"I don't know—whatever Emily told you." Henry went to the emergency department and checked for Arturo's X-ray report. Sure enough, broken nose and two broken ribs. No way the other guy wasn't just as guilty. Detectives Megan and Ron came out from Arturo's cubicle.

Megan said, "That must have been quite the fight. Anyhow, Rivera admits to taking the first swing, but frankly, we interviewed the guy in the flag t-shirt and he had nothing but a scratch over his eye. Nothing like your patient in there."

Detective Ron Wooster said, "And t-shirt guy is twice the size of your patient."

"I just got back the imaging report. He's got a broken nose and two broken ribs, just as I suspected."

"Are you keeping him here?" asked Megan.

"No, there isn't much we can do here for him. He needs to rest and give his body time to heal. He can do that at home."

After the detectives left, Henry checked in on Arturo. Looking at him with his slight build and short stature, he couldn't imagine what he was thinking taking a swing at some brute in a bar.

"Doctor, did you find out the damage?"

"Just like I suspected. The nurse will show you how to tape those two broken ribs, and she'll give you instructions on caring for the broken nose. Basically, you'll be icing it on and off, sleep with your head elevated, and follow up in a few days. Once the swelling subsides we'll be able to tell if you need further treatment. I'll write you a script for extra-strength Tylenol. No aspirin or it may start bleeding again."

"Thanks, Doctor. Am I going to be arrested?"

"That's not my department."

"I never drink on a week night, you know? If that witch hadn't been at the Outside Inn last night, I'd have never gone to the bar."

"You said something about her getting your sister thrown out of the country. How did Faith Maguire know your sister?"

"When the witch moved here with her kids she needed a nanny. She hired my sister. My sister loved the kids and never had a problem until around Christmas time."

"What happened around Christmas time?"

"Maria Luz suspected something funny going on with the little girl. The witch was forever dragging the kid to the emergency room."

"She thought Ms. Maguire was abusing the kids?"

"She didn't say in so many words, just that things didn't seem right."

"Did she confront Ms. Maguire about it?"

"Not directly. She spoke to someone at the Department of Children and Families, and Faith Maguire found out. Next thing we know, Maria Luz is picked up and sent back to Mexico, just like that. She was taking classes at the university. She wanted to be a lawyer."

"I'm sorry. Did she speak to an attorney about staying here?"

"She never had the chance, not to mention the money."

"Did she go back to your parents?"

"My parents died in the earthquake last year. Maria Luz found a cousin to stay with for now and she's cleaning houses to make money."

"I'm sorry. They aren't coming after you, are they?"

"No. My parents moved here to study. I was born while they were here so I have citizenship. Maria Luz was born after we moved back to Mexico."

"But you came back?"

"My parents wanted us both to study here. Maria Luz had a visa but it had expired."

"She should talk to a lawyer. There are lawyers who work pro bono—for free."

The nurse came into the cubicle. "We need you in room 6."

"Okay. Arturo, someone will be in with the instructions. Take care of yourself."

Henry went next door and helped a patient having a seizure. When he was finished, he had a few minutes to himself. Seizures—Mila Maguire. He grabbed a computer and typed in her name. Arturo's sister was right. Mila Maguire had been brought to the ER six times since last September.

"Dr. Fox, a patient is asking for you. He doesn't understand the follow up instructions."

Henry returned to the elderly man he'd seen this morning and clarified the discharge instructions. By the time he finished up, his shift was over and he headed back home.

Chapter 6

Henry got home before Emily and Maddy. He poured Meow Mix into Chester's bowl, then foraged through the fridge and pantry. He hoped to whip up a nice dinner and surprise his girls but wasn't having much luck. Spaghetti with veggie meatballs? He searched for a pot. They'd recently had the kitchen renovated and nothing was where it used to be. He heard the door open.

"Henry, I'm home," said Emily. She took off her coat and came into the kitchen. "Don't tell me you're cooking for us?"

"Nothing elaborate." Henry found a pot, filled it with water, and set it on the stove.

"We have salad veggies in the fridge. It'll be just great. Besides, it's not like we can hop over to Coralee's for dinner, is it?"

"Unfortunately, no."

"Poor Coralee is beside herself. I hope the police clear her place soon. She's losing business left and right. As a matter of fact, I stopped for coffee at the new place and the owner has a full house thanks to this scandal. What a way to drum up business."

"You're not suggesting the new owner had anything to do with this, are you?"

"Just grasping at straws."

"Remember Coralee's employee, Arturo Rivera? The one who made a scene at dinner about Faith Maguire having his sister deported?"

"Yes. I'm guessing he's a suspect."

"I treated him in the ER today. Last night he got into a bar fight."

"So he has a temper. He had means and motive..."

"Yeah, but he's a hot head. Poisoning the cheesecake took concentration and a level head, don't you think? Besides, I didn't get the feeling he was a killer, just a brother upset over losing his sister."

"I don't know what to think. The whole incident is surreal. It still could be a random act. No one has ruled that out." said Emily.

Maddy came in cuddling Chester.

"How was school today?" asked Emily.

"It was school. We had a moment of silence for Ava's mother."

"Ava wasn't in school, was she?"

"No. I texted her and she's with Tilly and Mila. Her Dad is here."

"I'm sure having her father here is a comfort," said Emily.

Henry salted the water and broke spaghetti into the pot. "Maddy, can you hand me a jar of sauce from the pantry?"

Maddy complied. "I hope he doesn't take Ava and Mila back to Georgia. Ava loves school and it sounds like Mila does, too. I forgot that Jessica is her teacher. I should call her."

"I'm sure she's heard, but she works with kids. Maybe she knows the right things to say to help Mila." Emily set the table, stopping when she heard a knock. "I'll bet it's Kurt. He has a knack for dropping by at meal time."

"That's because he takes Prancer for a walk at this time every day," said Maddy. Emily translated the comment into *haven't you figured out the pattern by now, dummy?*

Prancer was an affectionate Chocolate Lab. Maddy adored him; Chester, not so much. His usual reaction was to hiss, then run and hide. Sometimes he skipped the hissing and ran straight under Maddy's bed.

"Hey, Kurt. Come on in," said Emily. She was amazed that he was walking Prancer wearing only a flannel shirt. Kurt said growing up in Minnesota had hardened him to the cold.

"I went by Coralee's earlier and saw the police out front. Do you know if something happened?" Prancer licked Maddy's hand as she reached over to pet him.

"It's been all over the news. Faith Maguire, the new school superintendent, died after eating tainted cheesecake from Coralee's. We ate with her the very night it happened."

"Really? That's awful. What do you mean by tainted cheesecake? Sour milk or something?"

"No," said Emily. "Someone deliberately added an overdose of diabetes medication to her dessert. She took it home and must have eaten it later that night. The housekeeper found her in the morning."

"Do they have any suspects? That charter school tried to open but Maguire went all the way to the state board to stop it. Happened just last month. Lots of angry investors."

"Right now, Arturo Rivera, Coralee's handyman, waitress Summer Martin, and the owner of the new inn are in the crosshairs."

Henry came out of the kitchen. "The owner of Smyth Haven? When did she become a suspect?"

Emily said, "She's not, really. It's my own hunch. She had a lot to gain by hurting Coralee's business."

Kurt said, "Arturo Rivera? It ain't him. I know him. He's done work on my cabin and my rental place. He's a good guy."

Henry said, "Want to stay for dinner?"

"Nah, thanks anyway. I've got leftovers in the fridge."

"Dinner's ready," said Henry. "Come on, you can have your leftovers for breakfast."

Kurt grumbled. "I could do that. Whatcha got?"

"Spaghetti and salad."

"Meatballs?"

"Not real ones." Emily glared at him. "I mean, we have environmentally, cruelty-free meatballs."

"Kurt, have you heard from Chloe?"

"Yeah. She's getting started on her dissertation. She'll be home for a visit in the summer."

Emily said, "Picking a topic and getting it approved is the hardest part. If she has a good advisor it'll go smoothly."

"Hope so. The girl's always studying or writing every time I call. Let me try one of those fake meatballs." Maddy passed him the bowl.

"Do you think Prancer wants one?"

"That dog will eat just about anything. By the way, how's the cat café doing?"

"Great. All the original cats were adopted within the first few months and the turnover has continued to be quick. There are only four now, but it'll be kitten season soon enough. I'm going to promote the two for one concept. Adopt cat siblings, twice the fun. Something like that."

No sooner had they finished eating, Emily's phone vibrated. "It's Coralee." She stepped into the living room. "Slow down. Did you call the police? They talked to her? If it'll make you feel better, I'll be right there."

She went into the kitchen and ate the last few bites of dinner. "I'm sorry, but I have to run over to Coralee's."

"Do what you have to do," said Henry. "I'll put the leftovers in the fridge. You can heat up more later if you're still hungry."

She let Kurt out on her way to the car. Coralee had said the police took a statement. She wasn't sure what help she'd be, but she knew Coralee was falling apart over all this. That's what friends are for, she guessed. In her heart she knew Coralee would do the same.

When she got to the inn, Coralee was at the front desk. "Thanks for coming. Would you mind coming with me to talk to the guest?"

"No problem." She followed Coralee down the hall.

An elderly lady opened the door. "Is this your friend?"

"Yes, this is Emily Fox."

"Tova Rosenbloom. The police didn't take me seriously. I know I had another bottle of my medication in my suitcase. I always travel with extra."

"You told the police. What did they say?" asked Emily.

Coralee interjected. "He acted like she was a senile old lady. I don't think he took her seriously."

"He? That doesn't sound like Ron Wooster?"

"Of course not. The new rookie they hired," said Coralee. "I was thinking you and I could help Tova look for it."

"Are you here by yourself?" asked Emily.

"No, my son and his family are in the room next to me. They went out to the movies tonight. I told them I was too tired to go. Here, this is my suitcase where I keep my extra meds." She opened the zippered pouch and took out Excedrin, Cortaid Cream, allergy pills, and half a bottle of cough syrup.

"What's this?" said Coralee. She took out an empty prescription bottle.

"See? Those were my extra blood sugar pills but they're all gone. I know the policeman didn't believe me when I told him it was full when I packed."

Emily said, "Coralee, you shouldn't have touched it. Maybe there were fingerprints."

"The rookie picked it up with his bare hands. No gloves or anything. I'm not the first to touch it."

"Do you keep medication anywhere else like in your purse, or in the bathroom?"

She opened her purse. "Well, just some Tums and my blood pressure pills in here." She showed Emily a plastic pill case.

"If you kept your blood pressure meds in here, why not the diabetes pills?"

"I don't know. They were in the bottle in my suitcase."

Coralee said, "What about in the bathroom?" She opened the bathroom door and saw pills spilled on the counter. "Are these them?"

"No, those are my thyroid pills. The rest are in my make-up bag."

Coralee unzipped the bag to make sure the missing meds weren't inside. "I'll call the detectives tomorrow and get back with you," said Coralee.

"Thank you for believing me." She closed the door and Emily heard her attempt to get the chain into the latch several times before the jingling stopped. They went back to the lobby.

"What do you think?" asked Coralee.

"She seems a little..." She searched for a euphemism for senile. "She seems a little disorganized if you ask me."

"Well, maybe. It's just she was so insistent. Thanks for coming over."

"Anything you need, call me."

The bell over the door tinkled. A young man, his wife, and son came inside. The man said, "Is it too late to get some hot chocolate?"

"Nope. I always keep some hot chocolate in the kitch...in my room. I'll get you some. Emily, this is Tova's family."

"Nice to meet you."

"You know my mother?"

"I'm a friend of Coralee's. Your mother swears she had her diabetes meds stolen. She felt like the police didn't take her seriously, so I came over to help Coralee check it out."

The wife said, "Her diabetes meds?" She opened her purse and took out a pill bottle organized by day of the week. "You mean these?"

The husband said, "Mom has a touch of dementia. She doesn't remember what she took when. My wife keeps her pills and gives them to my mother on the correct schedule. The pills Mom has in her room are placebos, just so she can feel like she's in charge of them."

"But thanks for taking her seriously," said the wife.

"I'm glad you cleared this up for us," said Coralee. "In the morning, call the police station and tell them what you told us. Before they invest time into investigating her stolen meds."

"She had the police come out for this? I'll have to apologize to them."

Coralee said, "Why don't you go get comfortable in your room and I'll bring by some hot chocolate in a few minutes."

The father scooped up the little boy. "Thanks. If he stays awake that long."

When they were out of earshot, Emily said, "Mystery solved."

"Thanks again. I'll go work on the hot chocolate."

Coralee went upstairs to her room. Emily zipped her jacket and was about to go outside when another guest approached her.

"Excuse me, but I couldn't help overhearing. My friends call me Bear. I saw something the night the lady was killed."

"Saw something? Did you talk to the police?"

He cleared his throat. "Not yet. Anyway, I was taking a walk the night it happened and got back around dinner time. I saw someone suspicious peeking in the ground floor window. The one overlooking the golf course."

"Where the dining room is?"

"Yeah. I'll show you."

She zippd her jacket and followed him out to the porch. "Over there?"

"Yeah." He walked around the side of the inn with Emily behind him. He led her to the dining room window. "He or she was standing right here looking in."

"What time was it?"

"It was 7:28. I was determined to get to my room in time for *Jeopardy* so I checked."

"Can you describe the person?"

"He or she was wearing a hoodie with a puffy black jacket on top. I couldn't see the face, but he was shorter than me, not slim, unless it was the puffy jacket that made him look bigger than he was."

"Why didn't you tell the police?"

He looked at the ground. "I'm sort of hiding out here. My ex is after me for child support and I think she's got a warrant out for me."

"Seriously?"

"Please don't report me. As soon as I find a job I'm going to catch up, I swear."

Emily shook her head, then went over to the window. There were cigarette ashes on the ledge. "Was the person smoking?"

"Yeah, as a matter of fact."

Emily walked back around the side. "I'll keep your secret if you get the information to the police."

"I can make an anonymous call, but if they come snooping around, I'm outta here."

"Okay. That's valuable information. The back door to the kitchen is right around the corner from the window."

Bear went inside, and Emily headed back to the car, then turned around. It wouldn't hurt to check out the area around the back door. She jogged around the window to the back. She spotted cellophane on the ground, like a cigarette package wrapper. And something else. Metal. She picked it up. It looked like the metal grasp for a zipper. She put on her leather gloves and picked it up. In the morning, she'd take it right to the station.

Chapter 7

The next morning, Henry went to the hospital. Emily told him about the ashes on the window ledge and asked him to check whether or not Arturo smoked. Not that patients didn't lie about their bad habits, but he'd promised he'd check. He sorted through the records for Arturo's medical history. Yep. Arturo smoked.

While he was in the records, he thought he'd check one more thing. Faith's daughter, Mila. Had she been here before with her seizures? Did the housekeeper know what to do if she had another seizure? She didn't live with her father. Was he aware of how to handle a seizure? He searched…Mila Maguire.

He scrolled through. Six times. She'd been through the emergency room six times since last September. Various tests had been run but they were inconclusive. He hated feeling helpless when tragedy struck. Keeping on top of Mila's health was a tangible way to help. Poor little girl was going through enough dealing with losing her mother. Deep in his thoughts, Pat startled him.

"Hey, buddy. Going through records? Not busy enough for you in the ER?"

"I was just checking on a few things. Any progress on your proposal plans?"

"I was thinking maybe a fortune cookie with the ring inside. I could take her to…"

"To a romantic Chinese restaurant like China Dragon? The one next to ShopRite over in the strip mall? The one with the take-out counter in front?"

"I was thinking *Disfrutar*. She loves all things Spanish."

"Meh."

"Okay, okay. I'll go back to the drawing board."

"Coralee called Emily over last night. A guest reported her medication stolen, but it turned out to be a false alarm."

"I spoke to Megan this morning. She said they finished their investigation of Coralee's kitchen. It was clean. No other contaminated foods or ingredients. She can reopen the dining room."

"That's good. Coralee works hard to keep that place running and to support her and her son."

"Doesn't that son of hers have a real job yet?"

"I think he's taking classes at St. Edwards. I know he helps run the inn."

"I gotta get going. I have to write up my report on Faith Maguire so the police can release the body to the next of kin."

"Her parents?"

"The ex-husband. Megan said they couldn't find any living relatives other than the girls, of course. And they're under age."

Henry put on his white coat and went to work. He was surprised to see Arturo Rivera in the first cubicle.

"I didn't expect to see you back here."

"I know you said to let the swelling go down, but last night it started bleeding and I got worried."

Henry examined his broken nose and looked in his throat. "Have you been resting?"

"I had to go back to work. I was making repairs on the inn all afternoon."

"No physical exertion for a few days. And ice it through tomorrow."

"Can you write me a note?"

A note? Like for the teacher? He cleared his throat. "I'll say you need to rest and avoid physical exertion." He felt bad that Arturo worried Coralee would doubt him. "By the way, I checked your records and it says you smoke. You certainly shouldn't smoke with all the inflammation in your nasal passages and chest."

"I know. I'd pretty much quit even before the fight. Maria Luz was always on my back about my smoking."

"That night we saw you at the inn when we were having dinner, after you got upset with Faith Maguire, where did you go? The bar fight wasn't until much later."

"I was in my room trying to cool off. I stayed in until after the late news on TV. Then I went to the bar."

Henry scribbled a note. "You can give this to Coralee. No physical exertion for a few days. Maybe you can help her with paperwork or something."

"Gracias, Doc."

"And ice. Get ice from Coralee. Twenty minutes on, twenty off."

Henry went back to work, planning on putting in half a day. Later in the morning, Megan dropped by.

"Hi, Megan. Pat's down in the morgue."

"I know. I had to check a few things with you for the investigation." She showed Henry a report. "Arturo Rivera says you treated him for a broken nose and cracked ribs after the bar fight. The imaging confirmed it?"

"That's right."

"He told us he didn't leave the inn until about midnight, when he went to the bar and he sustained the injuries there."

"That's the story I got."

"And you're pretty sure the injuries were from the fight?"

"Yeah. Why?"

"We have him on CCTV leaving the inn around 7 p.m. and returning before 8 p.m. Then he left again around midnight. We're just confirming the injuries were sustained at the bar."

"He lied about leaving the inn earlier?"

"Yes, he did."

"Why? Do you think he went out, got the diabetes meds, snuck back into the kitchen and poisoned the cheesecake?"

"It fits the timeline. He didn't leave for the bar until hours later."

"Emily found ashes on the window ledge at Coralee's—the dining room window ledge. And a piece of a zipper."

"She called and told me. In the footage, Arturo is wearing a zippered ski jacket. We'd need a warrant to check, unless, of course, he cooperates."

"Did he have access to the medication?"

"We haven't found a link yet. Unless of course…"

"What?"

"In some countries, a lot of these drugs are over the counter."

"You mean like in Mexico? That's ridiculous. He'd have had to plan way in advance. Arturo's a bit of a hot head. And why medication and not just rat poison or anti-freeze?"

"I think the killer was hoping it would appear Faith died of natural causes, like a heart attack or something."

"Well, I don't think he's your guy."

"Then why did he lie about his whereabouts? Where did he go between the time he blew up at Faith and when he was in the fight at the bar?"

"Ask him."

"We will. Changing the subject, what can I bring for dinner tomorrow night?"

"Not cheesecake."

While Henry was at the hospital, Emily sat at her desk with a cup of coffee she'd toted from home in the travel mug that Maddy got her for Christmas. She stared at the mug. Didn't she read somewhere that coffee causes breast cancer? Wait. Maybe it was that coffee helped prevent cancer. Convinced it was the latter, she took a swig. She hadn't been able to focus at home, alone with her thoughts, and hoped a change of scenery might help.

Determined to focus, she finished the last of her revisions and sent her soon-to-be-published book back to her editor. Relief. Hopefully this would do it and the book would be on its way to publication. What next? Living in Sugarbury Falls had given her no shortage of book ideas. The recent murder could easily work its way into print. She'd have to see how the case progressed.

"Knock, knock." Nancy poked her head in. "What are you doing here so early?"

"I wanted to finish my book revisions and send it off before class."

"That's great. You sure put that book together quickly. Has Maddy heard from Ava?"

"Just that her father is in town now and staying with them at the house. What about Brooke?"

"She just texted me. There's a memorial service tomorrow."

"So soon?"

"Does seem rushed. Emily, are you okay? You look like something's bothering you."

"You can't say anything. If this gets back to Maddy she'll be worried sick."

"You know you can trust me."

"I got a call from my doctor. You know the mammogram I had last week?"

"Yeah."

"I have to go for more testing."

"Like a biopsy?"

"No, they said they needed a clearer view."

"That happened to me. It's not unusual. They just need a close up of a section, that's all. They can't tell sometimes if what they're seeing is dense tissue, a cyst, or nothing at all."

"Or a tumor."

"Emily, don't jump the gun here. Call and make your appointment."

"Okay." She picked up the phone. "I'll call right now."

Chapter 8

Emily tried to call the breast center several times but the line was busy. She promised herself she'd call tonight, knowing the center had evening hours. When she got home, Henry's Jeep was in the driveway and she assumed Maddy was home from school by now. Emily dropped her bag on the sofa and took off her jacket.

"Maddy?" No answer. She knocked on Maddy's door. "Honey, I was thinking we could bring food over to Ava's before dinner. Want to help?"

Maddy took out her air pods. "What food?"

"Baked Ziti."

"Mila doesn't eat dairy, remember?"

"You're right. I could make a Shepard's pie."

"I guess. I've got a lot of homework."

"Do your homework. I'll let you know when it's ready and we'll drop it off."

Henry was flipping through the newspaper when Emily came into the kitchen. She gave him a kiss. "How was your day?"

"Okay."

"I'm making a Shepard's pie to bring over to Ava's. Want to help?" Before he could answer, she handed him an armload of potatoes and the peeler.

"Guess I'll do the potatoes," he said.

"Peel, cook, and mash. Did you find out whether or not Arturo is a smoker?"

"I saw him today at the hospital. He admits to smoking, though he's been cutting back. Megan pulled the CCTV footage from the night of the murder. It shows him leaving the inn shortly after he stormed off, then returning soon after. Before we left. Then he went out again around 11 p.m. Arturo says he was in his room until he left for the bar around 11."

"So, he lied. He snuck out, got the drugs, put it in Faith's dessert before we were done with dinner."

"That's the implication, but it's a short timeline. He'd have to have known exactly where to get the drugs to get back in time. Besides, like I've said before, he's a bit of a hot head. If he wanted to kill Faith, I think he'd have slugged her right there in the dining room."

"Yeah."

"Yeah, what? You agree?"

"If he works at the inn doing handyman stuff, wouldn't he know Coralee had video surveillance?"

"You'd think so. Hey, did something happen at work? You seem distracted."

She really wanted to tell him about the mammogram, but she couldn't risk Maddy finding out. Besides, Nancy and the nurse who called both said it was probably nothing to worry about. "I'm fine." She stirred the ground beef in the pan. The longer she'd been vegetarian, the more she couldn't stand the odor of meat. When it finished cooking, she drained it and left Henry finishing the potatoes while she made her phone call in the bedroom.

Her fingers shook as she pressed the numbers. "Hello, this is Emily Fox. I need to make an appointment for a follow-up mammogram."

The receptionist seemed to have recognized the name. "Yes, Mrs. Fox. We got orders for a compression and an ultrasound. How's Monday at 2:00?"

"Fine. Um, do you get a lot of those call backs? Does it mean…"

"It just means the image wasn't clear for whatever reason and the doctor wants a better view. Don't worry. It's fairly common."

"Thanks. I'll be there on Monday at 2." When she went back downstairs, steam rose from the pot of potatoes. Henry had taken out a few cans of peas and carrots.

"Everything okay?"

"Just needed the bathroom. Think we'll have this together before dinner?"

"Yeah. What are we making tomorrow night?"

"I'm thinking vegetable lasagna and a nice salad. Megan's bringing dessert. Maddy asked if we could invite Jessica over."

"Great. I still can't believe she has a sister. The miracle of DNA testing gone commercial."

"Bizarre. Their father's sitting in jail. What an egotist, fathering all those children and his patients thought they were getting an anonymous donor."

"That could be your next book."

"No, it's open and shut. I need gray area to make it interesting reading."

"The potatoes are done. Let's put this together and we can relax while it bakes."

He and Emily sat in the living room. "I wonder about the owner of Smyth Haven. She's certainly benefitting with the negative publicity against Coralee's place."

"That's extreme, wouldn't you say? And besides, she snuck in just during that window of time to poison Faith Maguire?"

"The more I think about it, maybe Faith wasn't the target. What if Rona Smyth injected the cheesecake and didn't care who it killed. She could have done that ahead of time."

"You can ask Coralee if she'd ever come by the inn."

She opened her lap top. "Let's see what we can find out about Rona Smyth." She googled the name and sorted through information. "She grew up here. Then she moved away and had her own restaurant about an hour away."

"Is the restaurant still there? I wonder if she still owns it."

Emily googled some more. "I don't see it here. Wait, let me try something else."

"It could have changed names if she sold it."

"Look. Here's an article that says the restaurant caught on fire and was burned to the ground. It says the owner decided not to rebuild and moved to Vermont to be near her aging parents."

"There you go. She must have used the insurance money to renovate Smyth Haven."

"The timeline looks about right. I wonder if her parents still live here."

Emily searched the obituaries. "Smyth is a very common name."

"Narrow it down to our county and within the past two years."

"Here it is. Charlie and Joan Smyth died in a car accident about six months ago."

"How awful. She said they were elderly."

"Not so elderly. In fact, they weren't all that much older than we are."

"I guess age is relative. At least she got to spend some time with them before they died."

"Do you smell something?"

"The Shepard's pie!" She ran to the kitchen, followed by Henry and opened the oven. "Phew. It looks perfect. I'll let it cool."

"We can bring it over warm and they can have it for dinner."

"Good thinking. I'll get Maddy."

When they got to Ava's, Tilly the housekeeper answered the door. "You didn't have to bring food. How kind of you. Come on in."

Emily set the Shepard's pie on the table. "I thought if you hadn't made dinner…it's still warm."

"I hadn't even thought about dinner yet. Poor Mila's been crying nonstop. I just rubbed her back and got her to fall asleep. Maddy, Ava's in her room. Go on in, she could use the company."

A tall man in an Emory sweatshirt and jeans came into the room. "I'm Dave Maguire."

"Emily and Henry Fox. Ava's a friend of our daughter's. We ate together the night Faith died. I'm sorry for your loss."

"It was quite the shock. I'm glad I was able to get here right away for the girls."

Emily said, "I was glad, too. I heard they're having quite a blizzard in Atlanta. Did you fly through Atlanta?"

"Got out just in time."

"Do you think the girls will be okay? Are you taking them back to Georgia?"

"I haven't thought it out yet."

Tilly said, "They're more than half way through the school year. And Mila loves her teacher. It might be wise to let them stay here until school's out for the year."

"I've got a lot to think about. I've been working on the arrangements for the memorial service. Looks like we're clear for the day after tomorrow."

Emily wasn't sure she'd heard right. Did the police release the body already? "That's so soon."

Tilly said, "I got in touch with the minister from the church we've been going to with the girls. He's going to do a simple ceremony."

Dave said, "We'll keep the ashes in an urn for now. When we're settled, I'll talk to the girls and perhaps spread them over a favorite spot. Not that I know where that'd be, but Ava will have some ideas. I'm glad Tilly had connections."

"Ava was living with you, right?"

"Yeah. The high school was much better. Of course, that all changed when it became convenient to ruin my reputation and sever my custody arrangement. Everything was fine until I objected to her moving the girls out of state."

Henry said, "How are Mila's seizures doing?"

"She hasn't had any since I've been here. She never had one while I was with her, but, of course, that wasn't often. Even when I was supposed to take her for a weekend, half the time she was too sick to visit. She barely knows me."

Emily said, "You're her father. It won't take long to bond."

Tilly said, "Mila is upset, of course, but health wise she's doing okay. Do you all want to stay for dinner?"

"No, thanks," said Emily. "Maddy has a lot of homework. Let me know if you need anything and keep us in the loop about the memorial service. Ava knows how to reach us."

Chapter 9

Henry stopped by the hospital in the morning. He was going to put in a couple of hours, only because one of the doctors was on vacation. Normally he kept the weekends free.

Pat came up behind him. "Still on for tonight, right?"

"Of course. Are you up for a game of *Scattergories* after dinner?"

"Always."

"I thought you weren't working today?"

"I had to fill out the paperwork releasing Faith Maguire's body. The ex is very anxious to get her cremated. It gives me a bad feeling."

"Yeah, what's the rush? I met him last night and he already has a memorial service planned for tomorrow."

"They were divorced, right?"

"Yeah."

"Maybe he gets an insurance payout or something."

"There was a custody issue. Maddy's friend said something about how the mother severed custody ties before moving here."

"Think he did it?" asked Pat.

"Killed his ex-wife? He wasn't in town until after it happened. By the way, did you identify which diabetes drug killed her?"

"Yeah." He showed Henry the report. "This one. It caused her blood sugar to tank."

"It's a common medication. I've prescribed it myself a few times since moving here. It's quick acting."

"If we didn't test for it specifically, it wouldn't have been detected."

"I don't think Arturo Rivera is guilty. His actions that night are suspicious, but my gut tells me he isn't a murderer."

"Even though security cameras have him making a side trip right before the murder? A side trip he lied about?"

"Emily thinks maybe the owner of the new place, Smyth Haven, should be considered."

"I'm sure Megan and Ron have all the angles covered. By the way, is it just the four of us tonight? Megan's making dessert and asked me to find out if I saw you how much to bring."

"Maddy's half-sister is coming, too. And she might be bringing a date."

"So weird how Maddy connected with her, isn't it? That fertility doctor's in jail, right?"

"Yeah. What an ego. Fathering all those kids himself like that. Jessica found out through a DNA test, one of those they market nowadays. Shortly afterwards, the story broke."

"It's nice that she moved here."

"That was meant to be. She came to meet Maddy, and had just gotten her teaching degree. There happened to be an opening at the school here, which almost never happens."

"It's good she's got family. I mean, not that you and Emily…"

"I know what you mean. See you tonight?"

"We'll be there."

******

While Henry was at the hospital, Emily went for a jog around the lake. The weather wasn't perfect, but it was a little warmer than it had been and it wasn't snowing. She was so sick of the treadmill; she was willing to go out in a blizzard about now.

Rona Smyth. Her restaurant burned down, and she moved here to be with her parents, who died shortly afterwards. She must have used insurance money to renovate the place. As she came around the corner, she ran into her neighbor, Rebecca, walking her dog.

"Emily, I haven't seen you running out here in months."

"Cabin fever, I guess. I smell spring around the corner."

"Abby and I are going skiing later. It'll be probably the last time this season, even with the artificial snow."

"Did you hear about the murder?"

"Yeah."

"What can you find out about the owner of Smyth Haven?" She knew Rebecca's job involved tracking sensitive information that she wasn't able to talk about.

"I can find everything. Want to come inside?"

"Sure. Where's Abby?"

"Shooting engagement photos. She'll be back soon."

Emily followed her into the cozy cabin. Abby's photography decorated the wall over the fireplace. "Coralee is beside herself with the murder, even though it wasn't her fault. I had this idea that maybe her competitor, Rona Smyth, might be guilty."

"You just pulled that out of your head?"

"No. A guest at Coralee's says he saw someone peeking in the dining room window the night of the murder. There were ashes and a cellophane wrapper on the ledge and on the ground."

"And?"

"And Rona Smyth smelled like a chimney when I visited there."

"You know that she's not the only smoker in town, right?"

"Yeah, but she made a comment about her doctor telling her to watch her sugar. If she's taking oral diabetes meds, she had access."

"You know for sure she's diabetic?"

"No. Not for sure. And there were the galoshes by the umbrella stand."

"What about them?"

"They were still damp, and there was a reddish mud on them. Coralee has mulch outside the windows. The snow was melted enough the other day that the mulch may have been exposed."

"Let's take a look." She opened her laptop. "Spell the name." She typed some more. "Looks like she grew up here. I'll check the childhood address."

Within minutes, she had a picture on the screen.

"That looks like Smyth Haven. It's more rundown, and there's no porch but I think that's it. What's the address?"

Rebecca pointed to the screen.

"That's it."

"Were her parents living there up until they died?" asked Rebecca.

"I heard she inherited the place so I imagine they did."

Rebecca pulled up obituaries. "Yes, it says they resided there with their daughter, Rona Smyth." She continued her search. "She owned a restaurant before moving here. It burned to the ground."

"I heard."

"Hmmm."

"What?"

"Did you know the police suspected arson? They never could prove it. I've got two different newspaper articles that mention it."

"I didn't know that."

Abby came in toting a camera bag. "Hi, Emily. How's it going?"

"I've been trying to comfort Coralee. She feels so guilty about Faith Maguire's death, even though the police cleared her place."

"How's Maddy? She was friends with the daughter, right?"

"I think it's hitting close to home. Maddy's barely over the shock of losing her own mother. I feel bad for the daughters."

"How's your book coming along?"

"I sent in my revisions and now I need to figure out what I want to write about next. I'm at a loss."

Rebecca said, "This arson implication could be a story."

"It could. Where was the old restaurant?"

"Only about a forty-five-minute drive from here." She clicked a few more keys. "Here's a list of the people who worked for her with their last known addresses. You could start there. I'll print it off."

"Oh, and one more thing. There was a blizzard in the Southeast the day Faith Maguire's body was discovered. Her ex-husband arrived that night and he lived in Georgia. All the flights from Georgia go through Atlanta, right?"

"As far as I know."

"I'm not sure how he managed to get here that evening. From what I heard on the news, most flights were canceled."

"Give me a minute." She clicked some keys while the list was printing. "Some? All flights were canceled for a twenty-four-hour period. After that, of course, there were major delays in rescheduling flights. Here's a news clip from the Atlanta station."

Emily looked at the video. "People are sleeping on the floor of the airport."

"If Faith Maguire's ex claimed he arrived that evening, he's lying, or else he has his own private teleporter, like in Science Fiction."

"Rebecca, you're a miracle worker. I'm going to get busy doing some interviews. I don't suppose I could get the fire department's report?"

"Give me a little time. Right now, Abby and I are headed out to ski."

"Thanks. Have fun."

Emily went home and took a shower. Henry was delayed at the hospital, and Maddy went over to the cat café she'd founded over at the Outside Inn. She'd cleaned the house yesterday, and the lasagna wouldn't take long to make. She decided to do a little preliminary investigating. The list of Rona's past employees was still in her purse.

Chester, their black cat, was curled on top of the comforter. "What do you think, Chester? Should I make a few calls? Meow? Does that mean yes?"

The first few names on the list didn't pick up Emily's call. With caller ID, she didn't blame them for ignoring a strange number. She managed to connect on the next try.

"Hello, is this Shonda Riles?"

"This is she. I'm not donating money…"

Emily felt she was about to hang up. "No, I don't want money. I'm an author, Emily Fox. I write true crime books. I was wondering if I could interview you about the fire that occurred in a place where you once worked. I'm working on a book and could use your help."

"A book? What did you say your name was?"

"Emily Fox."

"I worked with Rona Smyth at her restaurant, The Silver Spoon. I could give you an earful."

"I heard the police suspected arson but couldn't prove it. What's your take on that?"

"It was arson all right. The Silver Spoon was headed into bankruptcy. Rona would have had to close the doors within weeks. Just so happened there was the fire and Rona collected a nice sum of insurance money."

"You think she set the fire?"

"The day it happened, she sent us all home early. She'd never done that before."

"In your opinion, was she the type of person who could torch her own restaurant?"

"Cold hearted witch. We all hated her. We all thought she did it."

"You've been very helpful. Are there others who you'd recommend I interview?"

"Yeah. Try Sue Simmons. She went to cooking school with Rona and Rona hired her as head chef. She'll tell you tales."

Emily checked the list and saw the name. "I'll try her. May I call you again if I need to?"

"You're writing a book exposing Rona? You bet you can call me."

Emily punched in the number she had for Sue Simmons. Disappointed at getting voicemail, she was about to hang up when someone picked up.

"Hello?"

"Ms. Simmons? This is Emily Fox. I'm an author doing research and was hoping to ask you a few questions regarding the fire at the Silver Spoon."

"Emily Fox? I saw you on a segment of *The Morning Show*. Ask away."

"Can you tell me about the night of the fire?"

"Well, the restaurant was empty, as usual. Rona sent us all home. The busboy was upset about losing hours but Rona promised we'd all be paid for the entire shift. We all left. In the morning, the story about the fire was all over the news. Police asked me and the others a few questions, and that's the last we heard. I assume Rona collected a hefty bundle of insurance money. More than the place was worth, which at that point was zero."

"Why was the restaurant in trouble?"

"Well, it certainly wasn't my cooking. The ambiance was dated. Rona hadn't kept up with repairs. The place was a fixer upper when she bought it and she never had the resources to get it up to speed. When a new place opened down the block with comparable cuisine at lower prices and a nicer décor, that was the beginning of the end."

"Do you think it's possible that Rona set the fire?"

"She'd do anything to save herself. When we were in cooking school together...well, I'd better not say."

"Please, go on."

"You should call Mary Burke. She works at a bakery. It's her story to tell. Gotta go, my husband's calling on the other line."

"Thank..." The line went dead. Mary Burke. She was searching for the number when Henry came home.

Chapter 10

"Maddy, can you get the door?" Emily pulled the vegetable lasagna out of the oven and set it on the trivet. "Henry, can you bring the cheese and bruschetta out to the living room?"

She followed him to the door a few minutes later.

"Emily, whatever you made is making my mouth water," said Megan. She handed her a bottle of wine, then looked at Maddy. "I'd have to check your ID before serving you."

Maddy giggled, which was a welcome sound to Emily. Since Faith's death, Maddy had been quieter and sadder than she'd been in a while. Maddy and Megan had connected right away when Pat started dating her and bringing her to the house. Megan was a little closer to Maddy's age, Emily guessed mid-thirties, and seemed to get the whole teenager thing better than she did.

The doorbell rang. "I'll get it," said Maddy, peeking through the peephole. "It's Jessica."

Jessica Pratt was in her mid-twenties, with long blond hair pulled into a high ponytail. If she looked at a certain angle, Emily could see the resemblance between the half-sisters, though Maddy's hair was darker, and Jessica had freckles across her nose.

Jessica introduced her friend. "This is Sam Benson. He teaches at my school."

Sam was older than Jessica—handsome, with lines across his forehead that crinkled when he smiled. "Nice to meet you. I've heard so many nice things about your family. Jessica is so happy to have found you, Maddy."

"Same here. She's the only family I have, other than my felon of a father, who I'd never expected to know."

Emily's hurt must have shown on her face.

Maddy looked at her and added, "By family, I mean blood relatives. Emily and Henry are my family. I'm lucky to have them."

Henry grabbed a corkscrew and wine glasses from the kitchen while Emily took the guests' coats. Maddy invited them to try the cheeses and bruschetta.

Emily said, "I hear you're Mila Maguire's teacher."

Jessica said, "Yes, such a sweet little girl. I was invited to the memorial service tomorrow. Her housekeeper said Mila wants to come back to school, but it's too soon if you ask me."

Maddy said, "She wants to feel normal again. When my mother died, I was so out of sorts. I craved the rhythm of my routine so I'd have less time to think about what I'd lost."

Emily remembered how Maddy tried to kill herself by taking an overdose after her mother died. That's when she and Henry made up their minds to accept guardianship and fly out to Chicago immediately. Maddy's days were anything but routine following her mother's sudden death.

Henry poured the wine. "Mr. Maguire didn't waste any time getting the body cremated and setting up the memorial service."

Pat added, "He kept calling the morgue, asking when the body could be released. The minute he got the go-ahead, the body was picked up. Even Megan thought it was unusual."

"Unusual, yes, but people deal with grief in their own ways. Maybe he thought it'd be best for the girls to have closure sooner than later."

"Closure? That'll take forever," said Sam. He looked down and shook his head.

Megan said, "Sam, how long have you been working at the school?"

"I moved here last summer and started this school year, just like Jessica."

"Where were you living before?"

"Florida. Got sick of the never-ending heat. When Faith Maguire became superintendent, she added a technology special for the elementary students. I saw the advertisement and snatched it up."

Henry said, "A technology special? What's that?"

"The kids from each class come to the computer lab once a week and I teach them how to research, type— even how to code. This generation has a natural inclination toward technology."

"So it's like taking art or music, right?" said Megan.

"Yes, exactly. They have art, music, and PE weekly as well."

"Sounds like Faith Maguire was making positive changes," said Megan. "What a shame she had so little time here."

Sam said, "I wonder who they'll get to replace her, especially in the middle of the school year."

Emily got up and brought the food to the table. "Dinner's ready. Come on in."

She and Henry served the vegetable lasagna and passed around the salad. "I made meatballs for us carnivores. Any takers?"

Jessica said, "I've stopped eating meat after talking to Maddy." She took a bite of her food. "This is fabulous. I'll have to get the recipe."

"Gladly. You know, Coralee's been adding vegetarian dishes to the menu at the inn. She's come up with some delicious meals. You should talk to her."

"I will. I hope she wasn't derailed by the murder."

"Coralee was upset, but she'll bounce back. Always does. I'm glad the dining room was reopened. Megan, am I right in thinking the killer snuck in and poisoned the cheesecake the night of the murder? If the police didn't find contaminated ingredients, it had to have happened after the cheesecake was made."

"We tested what was left of the cheesecake. It was all clear. The drug had to be concentrated just in that slice."

"So it happened between the time we ordered dessert and when it was served, right?"

"That makes the most sense. Arturo Rivera and Summer Martin were both at the inn at that time."

"Megan, what about Rona Smyth? I think she was at the inn that night, too."

Megan put down her fork. "What makes you say that?"

"One of the guests at Coralee's said he saw someone sneaking around. He was supposed to call into the tip line."

"Why didn't he come forward? We interviewed all the guests who were there that night."

"He had his reasons. Anyway, I saw ashes on the window ledge, and a cellophane wrapper. Rona Smyth smokes and she wasn't at Smyth Haven that night. She says she was visiting a friend."

"Emily, I'm surprised you didn't tell me."

"The guest was supposed to leave all the information. I guess he didn't follow through. I'm sorry."

"It just moves Rona Smyth on to the shortlist of suspects if it checks out that she was there that night. I'll go by and re-interview the guests in the morning."

Pat said, "Can you pass the meatballs? Did you make these, buddy?"

"Sure did. My own secret recipe. Meat and breadcrumbs."

"This may not be appropriate dinner talk, but I did the autopsies on Rona Smyth's parents after the accident."

"Accident?" said Jessica.

"The Smyths were going out to dinner when their car wound up in the lake."

Emily said, "Were the roads slippery?"

"No, as a matter of fact, it was summer and the roads were dry as a bone. I couldn't figure out why they didn't just swim to the surface. They both drowned."

"Both?" said Henry. "Neither made it out of the car and to the surface?"

"Nope."

"Really?" said Emily.

"They both had water in their lungs."

"The passenger too?" said Henry. "Did carbon monoxide leak in? That can happen to cars, right? They could have been unconscious when they hit the water."

Pat said, "Not unless they were in a closed garage. I looked for signs of head wounds or drugs but couldn't find any evidence to negate the cause of death being listed as drowning."

Megan said, "There weren't any skid marks on the road, either. No witnesses. It always bothered me, but the family didn't push for further investigation."

The glass window shattered. "What's that?" screamed Maddy.

"Everyone down," said Megan. She gave it a minute, then found the source of the shatter. It was a rock, crudely painted with a message. *Stay out of it.* Megan grabbed a napkin and picked it up. "Is everyone okay? Emily, do you have a freezer bag?"

Emily ran to the kitchen and returned with one. "Who did this? Who is the message meant for?"

"I'm police, so I suspect it was for me."

Pat said, "Then why didn't they throw it through your window. I think it's a warning to Emily and Henry."

Maddy said, "Is someone trying to kill us?"

Jessica put her arm around her. "It's probably just kids playing a prank. The police will take care of them." She looked at Megan. "She's safe here, right?"

Pat said, "I'll help you board up the window. Whoever it was wanted to scare you. If they'd meant real harm, they would have been more discreet."

"Like sneaking in during the night and poisoning our breakfasts? Thanks a lot, Buddy."

"I didn't mean…"

"I'll have a patrol car cruise the area tonight. Meanwhile, I'll check with your neighbors and see if anyone saw whoever did this."

"It had to have been Rona Smyth. I started asking questions about her, exploring an idea for my next book."

Megan said, "We'll run by Smyth Haven and see if she has an alibi. Meanwhile, did anyone hear a car pass by?"

"No, and I was sitting right by the window," said Sam.

"I didn't hear any car," said Pat. Emily and Henry shook their heads.

Megan picked up the rock. "This isn't paint. It looks like it was written with a Sharpie marker. I'll check outside."

Henry grabbed a flashlight. "I'll come with you." He followed Megan down the driveway, to the front of the cabin. "Throwing it from a car would have required incredible aim and strength."

Megan agreed. "Whoever threw it was close to the window. If they drove, they'd have had to have gotten out to throw it. Shine the light across from here to the window. See. Boot prints. I'll have an officer get an impression." Meanwhile, she took an unofficial picture with her phone. "Why don't you spend the night elsewhere. I'd offer, but my place is pretty tiny."

"I'll take them to Coralee's."

"It was probably just kids, but just to be sure."

"Kids? One set of boot prints, not sneaker prints. I don't see beer bottles on the ground. I didn't hear motorcycles."

"A bit stereotypical, wouldn't you say? Just to be safe, stay at the inn tonight. I'll get a unit over here and see what we can come up with."

Chapter 11

"Coralee, thanks for squeezing us in last night." Emily sipped her coffee.

"It's not like we're full. I'm glad you came here instead of Smyth Haven."

"Don't be ridiculous."

Henry came into the dining room. "I just talked to Megan. They didn't get any prints and none of our neighbors saw anything."

Coralee said, "You thought it was teenagers?"

"Megan said there were no similar reports filed. I'm afraid I have to agree with Emily. This is personal, probably related to Emily asking questions."

"I'm sorry. I never thought…"

"I didn't mean to blame you, Em. It does make you wonder if Rona Smyth was involved in her parents' deaths. Otherwise, why the warning?"

Maddy came into the dining room. "Did they find anything?"

"No, not yet. Coralee has blueberry French toast. That'll cheer you up."

"I'm not a little kid. Sugar isn't going to change how I feel. I'm worried that whoever came after Ms. Maguire will come after us next."

Henry said, "There's no reason to think that. This is more likely related to Emily's research, or it was a bunch of kids." He knew it wasn't kids, but Maddy didn't have to know that.

Coralee said, "Did you check on the cats?"

"Yes. I let Tito sleep with me last night. I just put him back in the cat café."

"The service starts at 1:00, right?" asked Henry.

"Yes. I'm surprised they got it together and sent out the info so quickly. It'll be a tough day for the girls."

Summer Martin came into the dining room. "Sorry I'm a little late."

Coralee said, "It's okay. Things are just now getting busier. Can you seat the guests who are waiting?"

"Sure."

Coralee went back to work. Summer Martin refilled their coffees.

Emily said, "I heard what happened with Harmon College. I work at St. Edwards if you need…"

"Thanks. You know, I'm not to blame. My parents didn't tell me what they were up to. My grades were good. I'm sure I could have gotten in without their help. In any case, I've forgiven my parents, but Faith Maguire had no business butting into this. Who was it harming if I took a place which I actually deserved at Harmon? I'm glad she's dead."

"So I guess you won't be at the memorial service," said Henry. Emily kicked his shin under the table. "Summer, cream always rises to the top. It's horrible what happened, but it doesn't have to destroy your life."

"We'll see," said Summer. She moved on to the next table.

Henry said, "I'm going to swing by the house. Arturo Rivera worked on Kurt's rental cabin as well as the inn. Kurt and Coralee were both pleased with the job he did. I'm going to see if he'll do the repairs."

"But he's a murder suspect."

"I don't think he did it. Besides, if we get to chat while he's repairing the window, if he's guilty he might slip and say something related to the case."

"I'm going to stop at Rebecca and Abby's. Maddy, want to come?"

"No. I told Coralee I'd help at the cat café. We're getting two new kittens that someone found by a dumpster."

"We'll pick you up before the service. Come on, Em."

Emily and Henry drove to the house. Emily said, "I'll walk over to Rebecca and Abby's and meet you back here."

"Insurance should cover the window."

"I'm not worried." She gave him a kiss. "See you in a bit."

Emily walked over to the girls' cabin. "Hey, thank you for following up, Rebecca."

"No problem. I found out Rona Smyth's restaurant was in the red, big time. She had started the paperwork to file for bankruptcy. The fire and insurance payouts were a lifeline."

"So it would make sense if she started the fire to collect the insurance."

"That's not all. Here's the report from the insurance investigator, and from the fire department. They don't match."

"What do you mean?"

"The original report says an accelerant was found at the scene and there was a likelihood of arson. The insurance report says the fire started due to faulty wiring."

"That doesn't make sense at all. The insurance inspector is the one who would want to deny a claim and say it was an accident or faulty wiring."

"That's what I thought, until I checked the bank records."

"How did you…"

"Emily, by now you know not to ask. The inspector deposited a large sum into his bank account the same day Rona withdrew the same amount from hers."

"But you said Rona was nearly broke."

"Look at the date. The payout was after the insurance company paid out to Rona. It must have been part of the deal. The inspector agreed to take the bribe after the company paid out."

"Wow. Even so, proving arson doesn't really help me. I can't base an entire book around it. In fact, it gives Rona less reason to murder her parents if she had the insurance money with which to renovate Smyth Haven."

"I'm still working on it. I'll let you know when I have more information. Oh, and here's a contact you might want to check out."

Rebecca handed her a paper. "Who is it?"

"This lady filed a civil suit against Rona back in their cooking school days. She accused Rona of, get this, tampering with her opponent's ingredients during a bake-off contest. Looks like the suit was dropped, but you should talk to this woman. Shows a pattern if it's true."

"You're amazing. The government should hire you to do espionage work."

Rebecca smiled. "You never know."

Emily got back to her house before Arturo left. "How's it looking?"

Henry said, "Arturo's fixing it for us. He ran over to the glass shop, picked up what he needed, and he's installing it now."

Arturo's jacket vibrated on the coat rack. Henry said, "Someone's calling him. Should I bring it to him?"

"They can leave a message."

No sooner had she said that, it began to ring again. "Persistent."

"It might be an emergency," said Henry. "I'll take it to him." He took the phone out of the jacket pocket. "It's an oldie. Guess Coralee doesn't pay him well."

"I don't know about that. He's driving a new truck. I'll bring it to him."

Emily ran upstairs to get ready for the memorial service. When she got out of the shower, she heard Arturo's truck pull away. Henry came upstairs.

"The phone call must not have been an emergency. I heard him pull away just now. Is the window fixed?"

"Good as new."

"Something's on your mind."

"When I brought the phone to Arturo, I noticed he had another phone sitting on top of his tool box. It was an iPhone."

"Well, what do you think he's up to with the second phone? Cheating on a girlfriend?"

"He didn't mention a girlfriend. The nurse asked if he wanted us to call someone and he said no."

"Maybe it's a work phone, so he can turn it off when he's off duty."

"Off handyman duty? I'd better get changed. We have to go. Is Maddy ready?"

"She's at the inn helping with the cats. I'll text her and tell her we're on the way."

The memorial service was just getting started when they arrived. They passed Coralee as they walked in. Ava, Mila, their father, and the housekeeper sat in the front row of folding chairs. Emily looked around and felt sad. Only half a dozen others, including Maddy's half-sister Jessica and the technology teacher, had come to the service. She guessed the others were work colleagues. Nancy and Brooke walked in and sat behind them. Megan and Pat snuck in just after the minister started the service.

The minister said, "Faith Maguire will be missed. She leaves behind two young daughters who will carry her in their hearts. In the short time she'd been in Sugarbury Falls, she was already making positive things happen in our school system. She will be missed, but know she's in the hands of our Lord and will enjoy everlasting peace." He led the group in a prayer and that was that. No music, no eulogy, no casket.

Tilly, the housekeeper, had set up a coffee urn and cookies at the back of the meeting room. Ava had been crying throughout the service. Emily gave her a hug.

"I'm so sorry about your Mom. If there's anything we can do, please ask."

Ava sniffled. "There's nothing anyone can do, except to catch her killer. Poor Mila is a wreck. She can't believe someone killed our mother."

Jessica Pratt approached them with Sam, the teacher she brought to dinner the other night. She bent down and hugged Mila. "Honey, I'm so sorry. I know you loved your mommy so much and she loved you with all her heart."

Mila cried into Jessica's shoulder. Tilly came over and scooped her up in her arms. "It's going to be okay, sweetie. I'm here, Daddy is here, and so is your sister. We're not leaving you."

Dave Maguire had been talking to the minister and now came over to them. "Tilly, you're so good with her." He introduced himself to Jessica and Sam.

"I'm Mila's teacher. I'll do whatever I can to make things as easy as possible when Mila returns to school."

"Thank you. Can I ask you something?"

"Sure."

"Has Mila missed a lot of school due to her health?"

"More than the usual, but she always makes up the work. Her health comes first."

Dave Maguire nodded. "I'm going to get the girls back in school as soon as possible while I figure out our next move."

Jessica said, "It's more than halfway through the school year. In my opinion, it would be helpful if the girls finished out the year and weren't uprooted right away."

"I agree," said Tilly. "But like I told Dave, I'm willing to move with them if he wants me."

"The girls are obviously attached to you, Tilly. That's a generous offer."

"Tilly, did you grow up here in Vermont?"

"No, I moved here around the same time as Faith and the girls. I'd recently gotten divorced and wanted a new start."

"You picked a great place for a new start."

"My family used to vacation here. It's always had a warm place in my heart."

"Were you in child care before?" asked Emily.

"Oh, no. I was a secretary at a health clinic. I have to say this is way more fulfilling."

Dave said, "We're all lucky to have her." His phone buzzed. "If you'll excuse me."

Nancy and Brooke, who had been speaking to the minister, came over and hugged the girls. "Ava, I'm always available. Call or text any time, doesn't matter how late."

"Thanks, Brooke. Can you and Maddy update social media and say I'm okay but need space? I can't deal with answering texts and keeping up with Snap Chat now."

"Of course."

"We'll be heading back now. If you need anything..."

"Thank you Mrs. Fox," said Ava.

"Text me," said Maddy. She hugged Ava.

On the way back, Emily said, "I think we're being followed."

"That's crazy. There aren't any cars behind us."

"Not a car."

At that moment, a motorcycle zipped past them and cut across the front of their car.

"Hang on!" Henry slammed on the brakes.

Chapter 12

"That was a close one last night," said Emily. "I hope the police caught the guy."

"I wouldn't hold my breath. By the time the police made it over, he was long gone. Maybe you should lay off the Rona Smyth story."

"You think that's what this is about?"

"Our window is busted, then the next day a motorcycle nearly kills us. Think about Maddy."

"If someone's trying to stop me from asking questions, then it proves there actually is a story."

"Look, you should stay away from Rona Smyth. If she burned down her own restaurant and killed her parents, let alone possibly poisoned Faith Maguire, there's no telling what she'll do next."

Emily looked at the rooster clock. "I have to get going." She gave him a kiss. "Make sure Maddy gets off on time. She's usually up by now."

"Where are you going so early?"

Emily slipped out the front door without answering. All she could think about was getting this appointment over with and getting a clean bill of health. She took a deep breath. Just seeing the pain in Ava's eyes and watching Mila's uncontrollable sobbing yesterday gave her the shivers. She couldn't fathom Maddy going through that...again.

She checked the GPS. Twenty minutes to the center. She put on an audio book but couldn't focus, so she switched to the radio. She was probably overreacting to this whole thing. Henry always teased her about jumping from A to Z.

All the police had to do was check to see if Rona owned a motorcycle. If she didn't…on the other hand, she could have borrowed one. Borrowed? Motorcycles were a rare sight in Sugarbury Falls. This was more of a bike or hike community. Rebecca would be able to find out right away. Maybe she'd stop by after her appointment.

Emily checked in at the desk and settled down with a month old *People* magazine. She flipped through the wrinkled pages, finding it hard to concentrate. Reporters got paid to write about Kardashian sightings? Probably more than she earned from years of work as a crime reporter. She checked the wall clock, then pulled out her to do list. After this, she wanted to contact Mary Burke, the name she'd gotten from Rona's acquaintance. What was taking so long? She'd been here longer than the two people who came in after her.

"Emily Fox?" The nurse stood at the door holding a clipboard. She followed her into a dressing room. "Wipe off your antiperspirant and put on the gown with the opening in front. The technician will come get you in a few minutes."

Emily did as she was told, carefully folded her blouse with her bra tucked inside, and sat in the plastic chair outside the dressing room. She wanted to get this over with and braced herself for the sure to be excruciating wait for results. Could she seriously hide this from Henry? He was sure to notice her anxiety. Maybe she'd just go ahead and tell him.

"Mrs. Fox, follow me." Emily shivered in the freezing cold mammography room.

"Stand on the tape, face this way, hold your breath."

The technician, satisfied with the positioning, stepped away and took films of the breast in question.

Luckily, Emily never found the mammography process to be painful, though several of her friends felt differently. After she was done, the technician pointed her in the direction of the ultrasound suite. One test down, one more to go.

"Just relax. This will feel a little cold." Emily, already covered in goose bumps, shivered more when the technician covered her breast with goopy gel. She turned her head and watched the image on the screen. Never having had children, she felt she'd missed out on seeing something interesting, like a fetus. Wait. Didn't being pregnant and nursing reduce your risk of breast cancer? The technician hovered over one spot.

"Why are you stopping?" She was sure the blob of white she saw on the screen was a tumor. She felt her hands clench.

"Relax. We take standard measurements."

People assumed she and Henry didn't want children. They were both somewhat older and at the height of their careers when they got married. And there was the death of her sister—she'd never gotten over feeling like it was her fault. Truth was, they'd tried but it never happened. She never told anyone how much they'd really wanted a baby. They'd even considered infertility treatments but by that time her age made the odds too bleak. The technician stopped again.

"Is anything there?"

"I'm not the doctor. I can't say. They'll contact you with the results."

Why couldn't she say? Surely she did hundreds of these and knew whether or not something looked amiss. She bet that if everything was normal, she'd have told her so, or at least she'd make a comment like 'don't worry, it'll be fine.'

"All done." She handed her a wipe. "You can get dressed and they'll be in touch soon."

Soon? Did that mean there was something that needed to be acted on quickly? Soon was so relative. A day? A week? Two weeks? She asked on her way out but the receptionist wasn't any more specific.

When she got to the car, she called Mary Burke. Mary Burke agreed to speak with her but was at work and wanted to talk in person. Emily got an address and headed to Mary Burke's bakery.

It would all be okay. She knew she tended to overreact. It was her way of dealing with the possibility of bad news. She imagined the worst and tried to convince herself it sounded ridiculous. Only this time, it didn't sound ridiculous enough.

She found a parking spot right in front of *Buy the Dozen*. When she smelled the fresh bread the moment she crossed the threshold, she realized how hungry she was. The cashier showed her to the kitchen, where Mary Burke was checking the inventory.

"Ms. Burke? I'm Emily Fox. Thanks for allowing me to come by."

"Not a problem. You said this had to do with Faith Maguire?"

"Yes. As I said, Faith Maguire was murdered last week. She'd eaten food laced with a diabetes drug at my friend's inn. My daughter happens to be friends with Faith's daughter. Anyway, I'm doing a little investigating to help the police find the perpetrator. I understand you knew Rona Smyth from back in school."

"Yes. We were," she cleared her throat, "friends. Or so I thought."

"What do you mean by that?"

"We both wound up in the finals for a national baking contest. It came down to the two of us. The day of the bake-off, we had to create a four-tier wedding cake. Hers was beautiful, I'll admit. Chocolate ganache.

Mine, however, was stunning. I watched the faces of the judges when I presented it. I replicated a chapel with stone steps made of marzipan and a stained glass window out of candy brittle. It was gorgeous. No contest."

"And you didn't win?"

"The judges got sick after just a few bites. Ran to the bathroom, all three of them. Of course, she won. After all, who votes for a cake that makes you sick, right?"

"But how..."

"I found out later she'd put drops of Visine into my fondant. I found the bottle in the kitchen trash and confronted her. She admitted it to me but, of course, wouldn't tell the judges."

"Why didn't you say anything? They could have sent the cake to a lab to be tested."

"By then, I'd dumped the whole thing down the garbage disposal. They wouldn't have believed me. I'd have come across like a sore loser."

"I'm so sorry."

"Yeah, well. She got a cash prize and a job offer. I got a bad reputation and here I am managing a bakery that's not even my own."

"That's awful."

"Can't say I shed any tears when I heard her place place burned down."

"Sure. Thank you for your time."

"No problem. Grab a pastry on the way out. It's on the house."

Taking the white bag, she replayed the scene Mary Burke described. Judges taking a bite of Mary's cake and rushing off to the bathroom. Nevertheless, once in the car, Emily demolished the sticky bun, licking the glaze off her fingers as she drove. She seldom allowed herself such an indulgence, but life was short. What? She couldn't start thinking that way.

Rebecca and Abby both worked from home. Abby was a photographer. Rebecca didn't ever define exactly what she did, but it had something to do with the government. In any case, it paid well. She and Abby had beautiful art-work and rugs in their cabin. Although they were the most down to Earth couple she'd ever met, they managed to travel extensively and had honeymooned in Bora Bora for six weeks.

When she pulled into their driveway, Abby was leaving with her tripod and camera bag in tow.

"Rebecca's inside. I'm doing a photo shoot for the Chamber of Commerce. I suggested filming in front of The Outside Inn, which they were all for until the bad publicity. This morning they called and said we're meeting in front of Smyth Haven."

"You're kidding. What a slap in the face for Coralee. The police already said they found no trace of it being Coralee's fault."

"I know. Totally unfair. If they catch the killer soon, maybe we can do the next one back at Coralee's. I hear they're planning on shooting a commercial."

"Maybe by that time Rona Smyth will be in jail." She didn't realize until the words left her mouth that she considered Rona Smyth her number one suspect. Perhaps Rebecca would solidify her theory. She knocked on the door.

"It's open," called Rebecca, who was sitting at the table with her laptop. She closed the lid when Emily came in. "Hey, Emily. Can I get you something to drink? You okay? You look stressed."

"I'm okay. I visited Mary Burke at her bakery job. Sounds like Rona was pretty evil. I wouldn't put murder past her. Can you find out if Rona owns a motorcycle?"

"A motorcycle?"

"Someone threw a rock with a warning through our window last night. We heard a motorcycle outside."

"Oh, no. Did anyone get hurt?"

"No, thank God. Can you find out?"

"Easy peasy. Give me a minute." She quickly got off the screen she'd been on and tapped at the keys. "Hmm."

"You found something?"

"No. I can't find a registration or a motorcycle license in her name."

"I suppose she could have borrowed one."

"I can't say I've ever seen a motorcycle around here. Snow mobiles and scooters, yes, but no motorcycles. I'd have noticed."

"Yes, you are. Can you check Arturo Rivera and Summer Martin?"

She clicked away. "No, neither has a motorcycle license or registration."

"How about Dave Maguire? It would be registered in Georgia."

"Hmmm. Don't see it."

"That's puzzling. Those are the only people I can think of who'd want to scare me away from finding the truth."

"I'll keep my ears open. Meanwhile, let me know if you need more help." Her phone buzzed. "It's my boss. Gotta take this in private."

"Of course. Thanks again."

Emily got back in her car for the short ride around the bend. When she got to her door, she found a note stuck in it. She pulled it out thinking it was a notice about repairing the water lines or an ad for food delivery. It was neither. It was like out of an old TV show. Newspaper letters had been cut out and pasted to form the note. *I warned you.*

Emily fumbled with her key, locked the door behind her, and called Henry.

"Emily, stay there with the door locked. I'm coming home. Call the police."

"I will. Hurry."

Chapter 13

Emily paced and repeatedly looked at the window. Henry pulled into the driveway followed shortly by the detectives.

Detective Megan pulled out a notepad. "Tell me exactly what happened, Emily."

Emily picked up the note she'd put on the coffee table. "I got home and found this stuck into the space between the door and the frame. I thought it was an ad or something. I'm sorry, I touched it without wearing my gloves. I'll bet I ruined any chance of getting prints."

Megan said, "The person who wrote this took the time to hide his handwriting or printer by cutting out those letters. I'm sure he didn't leave fingerprints. Where were you coming home from?"

"I was over at Rebecca and Abby's."

"Did you pass anyone on the way? Did you hear anything unusual?"

"I didn't hear a motorcycle go by like I did last night. Not while I was at Rebecca and Abby's. I didn't see anyone on the way home, or at least I didn't notice anyone." She had an eye for noticing details but knew she'd been distracted over her mammography appointment. She could have missed something.

Henry jumped up when he heard a knock. Megan said, "That must be Ron."

Carrying an iPad, Ron Wooster said, "I talked to your neighbors. Kurt Olav was walking his dog and saw someone in a ski jacket run past them."

"Was it a woman?" asked Emily.

"He thinks it was a young man, but says he can't say a hundred percent."

"Arturo!"

Henry said, "You can't jump to conclusions. Besides, Arturo took a hard hit at the bar. Not sure he'd be running like that."

"We'll check it out. Meanwhile, stay alert and call us if anything else happens."

Emily locked the door behind them. "Henry, do you have to go back to the hospital?"

"No, they have things covered."

"Want to…"

"Go to the inn? Sure, why not." Henry grabbed his coat and keys. "I don't want Arturo to feel like we're spying on him."

"We won't be. Not really. Come on."

When they pulled up to Coralee's, there were fewer cars than Emily could ever remember seeing. "Coralee is really taking a hit. I think Smyth Haven is undercutting her prices and now with the murder…"

"It will be solved soon and the novelty of Smyth Haven is going to wear off."

"The Outside Inn is homier than Smyth Haven and Coralee beats Rona Smyth hands down in the hospitality department."

"She'll come out on top. Come on." Coralee was reading a paperback at the front desk.

"Emily and Henry? What are you doing here in the middle of the day?"

"Someone stuck a warning note in our door. Emily found it when she got home."

"A warning? Oh, Emily this just keeps getting worse. What did it say?"

"It tried to discourage me from getting involved, that's all. Is Arturo working today?"

"Yes, he's got a list of minor repairs to do. Handles on cabinets, spot painting, he said he wasn't supposed to do anything too strenuous."

"That's right, he's not. Was he here all morning?"

"As far as I know. I didn't see him leave or anything. He doesn't have classes today."

Emily said, "But he could have slipped out when you weren't looking, right?"

"You can't think Arturo left a threatening note."

"Kurt saw a young man around our place this morning while he was walking the dog."

"I doubt he even knows where you live. I can call him down here if you'd like?"

"Yes…"

Henry said, "No, we don't want to tip him off. The police may be coming to question him."

Emily remembered Bear, the guest who had helped her last time. Perhaps he'd seen something. "Is Bear still here at the inn?"

"Yes. He said he was going for a hike. Took his fancy camera with him."

"Hike? Do you know where?"

"The easy trail that starts out back."

"We'll be back," said Henry.

With spring around the corner, the muddy trail, no longer snow covered, was prime medium for footprints. Henry and Emily followed the path until they came upon Bear taking pictures of the lake.

"Pretty, isn't it?" said Emily.

Bear said, "I didn't hear you come up behind me. Yes, it's beautiful. All the postcards show this lake in the summer full of small boats or in the winter full of skaters. I like how it looks now—just pure nature."

"I agree," said Emily. "I jog around the lake and with the sun rising over the water, it's breathtaking."

Bear looked at Henry. "Bear, this is my husband, Henry."

He extended his hand. "Nice to meet you. You two out for a mid-day hike?"

"Actually, we wanted to talk to you. Remember how you said you saw someone peeking in the window at the inn the night of the murder?"

"Yeah. You kept my name out of it, right? I'll never sell enough photos to make up the alimony I owe."

"Of course I kept your name out of it. A reporter, even a retired one, never gives up her source."

"Can I help you with something else?"

"Hopefully. Someone threw a rock through our window the other night and today left a threatening note stuck in our door. Did you notice anyone—the handyman, in particular—leave the inn today?"

"The handyman? You mean the Spanish guy who changes the light bulbs?"

"Hispanic guy. Yes, Arturo Rivera."

"I've been out and about since breakfast. When I left, he was fiddling with the window locks in the dining room. I was out on the golf course taking pictures most of the morning. He didn't go out the back way like usual or I'd have seen him."

Emily said, "The back way? Like usual?"

"Yeah. My room overlooks the golf course. Sometimes I see him out smoking by the dumpster. Nearly every night I see him slip out carrying a box or a couple of garbage bags full of something."

"Did you tell the..."

"Police?"

"Yeah, I forgot. You're dodging your ex-wife. What time does he do this?"

"After dinner. Then he comes back maybe an hour or so later. It's not a crime, is it? Live and let live. It's not my business."

Henry said, "Do you have any idea what he's carrying?"

"Don't know and don't care. Like I said…"

"Yeah," said Henry. "Live and let live."

Emily was about to nudge Henry to go back to the inn, when she had a thought. "What kind of jacket does he wear when he goes out?"

"I seen him smoking wearing shirt sleeves, but when he does his nightly trip, he wears a ski jacket."

"A puffy jacket? What color?" She wondered if it had a broken zipper that matched the bit she'd found.

"Puffy? I don't know, just a ski jacket. Dark blue, with a hood."

"You're sure? Blue. Could it be black?"

"I suppose. Pretty sure it's blue though." He turned around sharply. "Did you hear that?"

"Hear what?" said Henry. He was losing patience with this conversation.

"The sound. I think it's an eagle." He pointed at the top of a tree. "See, there. Vermont is taking the lead in bringing back the bald eagle population." He aimed his camera and clicked away.

Henry said, "Go for it. We'll be heading back now."

"Thank you," said Emily.

"Yeah. No police, remember?"

"Got it."

Emily grabbed Henry's hand. "We should do this more often."

"What? Question witnesses about murder suspects?"

"No, take walks together. When we decided to semi-retire and move here, we said we wanted more time to enjoy nature and spend time together. Seems like we're almost as busy as we were."

"I never expected us to get involved with murder investigations. You can blame your friend Susan Wiles for lighting that fire."

"You enjoy the puzzle as much as I do."

"Yeah, but if I want to solve a puzzle, I can do my Sudoku."

"Whatever you say." She squeezed his hand. "Did I ever tell you how glad I am to have found you? Not everyone finds their soulmate."

"Where's this coming from?"

"Nowhere. I mean, I guess it's the moment, being out here with you on a beautiful day in a beautiful place."

"Hey, I have an idea."

"Do this more often?"

"No. I mean we can. I was thinking of something else. Pat's going to propose to Megan."

"What? You didn't tell me! That's great."

"You can't say anything. He's already got the ring. He wants the proposal to be special."

"A picnic out here would fill the bill," said Emily.

"Romantic, right? I'll suggest it to him."

"How exciting. Pat hasn't been this happy since Carol died. She'd want this for him."

"It's about time, too. Carol was his soulmate, blah, blah, blah. Eventually, you have to move on with your life."

"So if I died, you'd find a replacement?"

"In a heartbeat. Before your body turned cold."

She stared at him, mouth hanging open.

He squeezed her hand. "You know I'm kidding. What's with you today?"

"Well, I'd want you to be happy. The sooner the better. And Maddy needs a mother."

"Emily, what's going on? This doesn't sound at all like you."

She forced a smile. "I'm just yanking your chain. Come on. It's getting cold out here."

Chapter 14

"Emily, you ready?"

She wrapped her scarf around her neck. "Yes, all set. Maddy's doing her homework. I told her we'd be back in an hour or so." She locked the front door. The temperature had dropped significantly since their earlier walk.

Henry started up the Jeep. "I don't believe Arturo's guilty."

"Then we will be able to eliminate him. You have to admit he's up to something."

"Maybe he goes walking after dinner."

"Carrying a garbage bag or box? What if he's stealing items from the guests and reselling them?"

"If he was stealing garbage bags full of stolen items every day, don't you think someone would have noticed by now? I don't think he's our guy. It's someone else."

"Well, if it's not him, Rona Smyth is on my radar. Back in her school days, she tampered with her competitor's cake in order to win a baking contest. Her ex-employees from The Silver Spoon think she set fire to the restaurant to collect the insurance money. Oh, and she may have killed her own parents."

"There you go. Keep brainstorming."

"Summer Martin. Her whole future was derailed by Faith Maguire. Her parents are sitting in jail for bribery, and instead of enjoying freshman year at Harmon College, Summer's waiting tables and living in a hotel room."

"What do you think about the girls' father?"

"Dave Maguire? Faith says he was abusing the girls and got full custody away from him. True or not, he had to be furious. And I don't know how he managed to get out of Atlanta when all the flights were canceled due to the snowstorm."

"Let's park here. We'll be able to see Arturo leave."

"Should we slink down like we're on a stake-out?"

"Only if you brought food. It's almost eight o'clock now."

"Look, is that him?"

"Wait. Yes, it is. And he's got a box with him. Get down." He peered over the windshield. "Blue ski jacket. He's going to his car."

As soon as Arturo pulled out of the parking lot, Henry turned on the engine and followed, keeping a safe distance. He drove through the dark woods, following the narrow, twisty road. "He's heading to the river. Nothing good happens by the river at night."

"Look at all those homeless people under the bridge. It's so sad." Emily turned up the heat.

"The city chased them out of the park near the town square. Said it was bad for tourism, remember?"

"Yes. Many people are one paycheck or one medical emergency away from winding up homeless. They aren't all druggies or alcoholics, or mentally ill."

"Even if they are, they deserve a life-line. Come on. It looks like he's parking."

"Need these?"

"Binoculars? When did you get those?"

"Amazon. I saw Rebecca had a pair sitting on her table and I got inspired. Who knows when I'll want to go eagle-watching? Besides, if we ever take that Alaskan cruise, we can use them to spot whales."

"Look, there's an Orca. Over there, on the other side of the river."

"Very Funny." Emily scanned the area with the binoculars. "Arturo is holding the box. Two men are walking toward him. Arturo is handing them money. Now, the men have the box and the money. They're walking back to where they came from. Arturo's heading back to his car. What should we do?"

"That was a drug deal, I'm betting."

"Then why did the men get the box and the money, while Arturo walked away empty handed?"

"We should call the police."

"And say what? We followed Arturo and saw him handing a cardboard box to a couple of homeless people?"

"Then let's talk to Arturo. Come on, let's follow him back to the inn."

"Wait. He's going to deny everything. We have to catch him red-handed. Tomorrow, let's see if we can find out what he's taking from the inn and confront him before he leaves."

"Okay. We can even have dinner at Coralee's beforehand."

"Do you think Maddy's still up?"

"I don't know." He pulled into the driveway. "The light's still on in the living room." Maddy and Chester were cuddled together on the sofa, fast asleep. Henry picked up Maddy's geometry book which had fallen onto the floor beside her.

Emily tucked the afghan around her. "She looks so young lying here. Do you ever wonder what it would have been like had we been able to conceive back then? What it would have been like to raise a child from day one?"

"I used to think about it every time we saw anyone with a baby. As time went on, I accepted I was never going to be a father. Then along came Maddy. I

102 The Tainted Course

couldn't love her more if she was our own flesh and blood."

"I feel the same way, only..."

"Only what?"

"I've wondered how it feels having a baby move inside you. What's it like, being there the moment your kid takes his first breath?"

Maddy stirred. "Emily? Dad? What time is it?"

"Late," said Henry. "Why don't you go on to bed?"

Maddy slowly worked her way to sitting. "I will. I'm going to text Ava, first. She's worried her father is going to move them back to Georgia."

"Poor thing. How's her little sister doing?" said Emily.

"Ava hasn't said anything so I guess she's okay."

"Goodnight, honey. I'll make waffles in the morning so be up in time to eat them before school."

"I'll try." She scooped up Chester and went to her room.

"Em, I'm tired myself. Are you coming to bed?" He headed to the ladder.

"I'll be up in a minute." She went into the kitchen and made a cup of herbal tea. She hoped they'd have answers about Arturo after tomorrow night. Meanwhile, The Rona Smyth story nagged at her like a whiny puppy. How could she have orchestrated killing her parents? She'd have to have known how to tamper with a car. Even if Rona was innocent of killing Faith, the mystery surrounding her parents' deaths was one juicy story in itself.

Chapter 15

Emily grabbed the morning paper and sat down at the table with her coffee. The aroma of fresh waffles reminded her of Mary Burke's bakery.

"Do you want berries on these?" asked Henry. "They're not nearly as tasty as the ones we get in the summer, but they'll do for now."

"Sure. Should I get Maddy up?"

"I heard the shower when I came downstairs. She'll be in soon."

Emily picked up the newspaper. "Isn't that the mayor?" She held up the front page for Henry to see. "See the smiling guy in a hardhat breaking ground? Looks like that charter school Kurt was talking about is moving forward after all."

"Kurt said Faith Maguire was the only thing standing in the way."

"I don't know why we need another school in town. The public schools aren't over-crowded like in some areas of the country."

"When there's money to be made, that's reason enough. Maddy, want some waffles?"

Maddy had come into the kitchen. She put down Chester and filled his water bowl. "That's why I'm up. I smelled them from my room." She handed Emily a folded paper.

"What's this?"

"An invitation to the Science Fair. My project made the finals."

"I'm so proud of you, Maddy."

"The project I helped you with? Hope you gave me credit," said Henry.

"Yes, I could never have planted those beans without your help."

"Now you're being sarcastic," said Henry.

"Ava's project made it also. She built model houses out of different materials to see which would hold up better during a blizzard. She even made tiny windows out of glass. You should see it."

"I suppose we will." Henry took the paper from Emily and pulled on his glasses. "Friday night, in fact."

"Is Ava back at school?" asked Emily.

"She's coming back today. Jessica said Mila came back yesterday and she seemed all right."

"Getting back into her routine might be good for her. I can imagine sitting at home all day just gives them more time to think about their mother. Not that they should forget her, certainly. I mean, even though she's gone I'm sure she'll always be alive in their memories."

"Whatever. I have memories of my mom but I've forgotten a lot as time passes. Like how she used to make smiley faces on my pancakes. I thought of it when Henry was pouring the syrup just now."

Emily held back tears. She couldn't remember little details about her sister after all these years. If she died, Maddy would move on. They'd barely had time to make memories together.

"Em, you okay?"

"Yeah, why?"

"I don't know. Your expression. You looked so sad all of a sudden."

"I'm fine. Maddy, you should get going The bus will be here in a few minutes."

Maddy gobbled down the last of her breakfast and put the plate in the sink. "See you later."

Emily called after her, "By the way, we're having dinner at the inn tonight."

Henry put the leftover waffles in the fridge. "I'd better get going, too." He kissed Emily. "Have a good day."

Emily's class wouldn't start until mid-morning. With the house empty and a little time on her hands, she took out her laptop and searched for information about the crash that killed Rona's parents.

Rona was an only child. No wonder Megan said no one pushed for further investigation. It didn't add up. Her parents were found with their seatbelts on, the roads were clear, no skid marks. The airbags didn't inflate. Why not?

To top it off, Rona's restaurant had burned to the ground and she'd just moved home recently. Perfect timing. The parents die, the family home becomes hers, and the insurance money from the fire shows up in the nick of time to renovate the family home and turn it into Smyth Haven. Chester walked over the keyboard. She scooped him up and put him on the sofa next to her.

Pat had performed the autopsy, he mentioned it at dinner the other night and she asked if she could see the report. She grabbed her phone.

"Emily? Yes, I have some time this afternoon if you want to come by."

"I teach a class this morning but I can be at the hospital early afternoon."

"Great. I'll be here. I'll dig up the report and look it over again."

Emily smelled a story here. She wished her editor would call and say the final version of her recent manuscript was ready to go to publication so she could plunge into this next project. Could she get the police report for the accident? She'd check with Megan later.

Now she needed to get out of her pajamas and ready to teach.

When she got to her office, she organized the ever expanding piles of assignments she had to grade and picked up her red pen. She was shoveling as fast as she could, but the snow kept falling.

"Knock, knock. You busy?"

"Nancy? No, come in. Is that a new blouse?"

"Yes. Brooke and I hit the outlet mall last weekend. It's not too young looking, is it?"

"Of course not. The color matches your eyes."

"I hear Maddy's project made the finals of the science fair. Are you going Friday night? Brooke's made it, too."

"Of course, we'll be there. I hear Ava's going back to school today."

"Brooke said between the housekeeper and her father, Ava feels smothered. They're hovering over the girls."

"That's understandable. I'm glad their father got here so soon. Do you think he actually abused Mila, like Faith told the court?"

"Brooke said Ava told her Faith made it all up to get custody away from him. He was protesting her moving out of Georgia with the girls. According to Brooke, Ava adores her father."

"I'm glad he didn't really hurt Ava. What a shame, Faith discrediting him like that. And didn't she say Mila hardly knew him because she was always sick when she was supposed to go with him?"

"I don't know. Hey, did you go to your appointment?"

"I did."

"And?"

"And I have to wait until they call with the results. You know how bad I am about waiting for anything let alone something this important."

"It's going to be fine, you'll see." Nancy checked her watch. "I have class in a few minutes. We'll talk later."

"Bye."

Emily grabbed her things and made her way to her class as well. The topic for the day was writing true crime without getting sued. She'd learned all about it during her reporter days and was eager to share practical advice with the class. Afterwards, several students surrounded her and continued asking questions. When she finally broke away, it was later than she'd planned. She hoped Pat was still available.

When she got to the hospital basement, the door to the morgue was partially open. The smell brought back unpleasant recollections of dissecting frogs during high school biology lab. "Knock, knock."

"Come on in, Emily." He looked at her and must have noticed the smell bothered her. "We'll go in my office."

"Sorry I'm late."

"Not a problem. My patients don't complain about waiting. One of the reasons I love my job."

"I know we talked some about the accident that killed Rona Smyth's parents at dinner the other night. I'm pursing the story for my next book. You said they drowned, right?"

"Yes, there was water in both sets of lungs. No scratches or wounds like they tried to escape once the car went into the water. Seatbelts were still on. No burns or bruises from air bags. You know those things don't inflate without leaving a mark."

"Was it an older car? Perhaps it was before cars came with them."

"I don't know."

"Wait, I read the article in the paper. The car was nearly brand new. No drugs in their systems? No medical history?"

"None. I've worked on plenty of accident victims and their deaths didn't add up."

"Why did you sign off, then?"

"No one challenged the idea that it was an accident and the police seemed anxious to wrap it up."

"Rona didn't question their deaths? Did she have this information?"

"She did. In fact, I called her to ask a few questions. I wondered if there was a recent change in medical history. She said there wasn't and accepted my report at face value. If those were my parents in that situation, I wouldn't have been satisfied, but she was. In fact, I think it was her pressing the police to close the case."

"Did anyone check the car for what went wrong?"

"I don't know. I assumed the water damage made it difficult to examine."

"Thanks, Pat."

"Don't mention it."

"By the way, I hope you don't mind that Henry shared your plan to propose to Megan. I'm so happy for you."

"Thanks. I'm trying to plan a memorable proposal but I'm coming up short of ideas."

"Henry and I took a walk on the trail that starts outside the golf course. It's beautiful by the lake. Maybe a picnic. At sundown."

"Maybe. I'll check it out. Thanks."

In the car, Emily tried calling Megan to see if the Smyth's car had been examined after the accident, but she was unavailable. As she passed by an auto parts store, she had an idea. Her mechanic's shop was just down the road. He might have a few answers.

Nothing like the sight of grease stained jumpsuits on manly men, and the smell of new rubber tires. Even so, the auto shop was 'woman friendly', as Emily liked to say. Not that it took much, but it had lavender air freshener in the bathroom and a few issues of *Family Circle* in the waiting area. She'd once suggested a cappuccino machine, but Mac, her mechanic, just laughed.

"Emily? Do you have a problem with the Audi?"

"No, it's a dream to drive. Everything's good. I had a few questions to help with research for a book I'm writing."

"Ask away. Hope you don't mind, but I've got to continue working on the Chevy over there. The owner's coming at the end of the day and expects the repairs to be finished. Come on."

Emily followed him to the old Chevy with the propped-open hood. Even with the feminine touches, she truly hated auto shops. She got a whiff of burned oil as they walked.

"What do you want to know?"

"If someone wanted to rig a car so it looked like an accident, how would they do it?"

"You writing a thriller?"

"Something like that. Suppose a car goes off the road without leaving skid marks and heads straight into a lake. The victims have no marks indicating an effort to escape, and the airbags don't deploy."

"That could be a few things. Maybe someone cuts the brake lines, or messes with the steering mechanism. No skid marks indicate faulty brakes."

"Is that easy to do?"

"If someone knows about cars, then yes."

"And the airbags? Can they be switched off?"

"Yeah. They can also be removed, though who'd do that. Unless, of course, they wanted to kill someone." He chuckled at his own joke.

"Do you need specialized tools? Would it take long to do?"

"Nothing fancy. If someone knew what they were doing, it'd take no time at all."

"You're a big help, Mac."

"Can I be in your book?"

"You'll certainly be in the acknowledgments."

Chapter 16

Emily and Henry hadn't eaten at the inn since the night of Faith's murder. They were seated at the table next to the one they'd shared with Faith and her girls, making Emily feel a little out of sorts. She considered asking Coralee if they could move to another table, but Maddy didn't seem bothered and she preferred not to call attention to that night.

Henry said, "I'm getting the pot roast. You girls going to go carnivore? Just one night..."

"Dad, that's not even funny."

"You don't know what you're missing."

Emily said, "I saw a vegetable frittata on the menu. I'm going to have that with a salad."

"And I'm in the mood for a veggie burger. Settled," said Maddy.

Coralee came to the table. "Glad to see you back here. Business has started to pick up."

"I'm glad. Isn't that Summer I saw going into the kitchen?"

"Yes. She and Arturo are both working today. I've got him cutting veggies in the back. Are you sure the frittata is enough for you for dinner?"

"I'm not super hungry."

Henry said, "Maddy is a finalist in the school science fair."

"That's great, honey. Starting the Cat Café, winning the science fair...you'll be snapped up by any college you want to attend."

"I still have another quarter and then two more years before I'm there. After dinner I want to see the new kittens that were dropped off."

"They're adorable. It'll be hard for you to resist bringing one home with you."

Emily said, "I don't think Chester would welcome the competition."

"Your food will be here shortly. Enjoy."

Emily hadn't thought about Maddy leaving them for college.

"Maddy, do you want to go out of state for college?"

"I don't know. I haven't thought about it yet."

Henry said, "Depending on what you want to major in, you'll go to the best place you can get into. I'm thinking Ivy League. Harvard isn't too far away."

"If I don't get high enough SAT scores, will you bribe the head of the admissions committee for me?"

"You won't need it. Besides, I doubt I have a big enough bank account to cover what it would take to influence their decision."

The food came quickly, as promised. After dinner, Maddy headed upstairs to the cat café, and Henry motioned for Emily to follow him.

"Let's go around back and peek in the window." Henry led the way. "He's chopping vegetables. Wait, now he's taking off his apron. I think he's going down to the cellar."

"We can access the root cellar through those big doors in the ground. I hope they're not locked." She pulled the handle. "It's open." She led the way down the concrete steps. She coughed from breathing in the heavy, damp air. With each step it was darker and more difficult to see. She felt a spider web graze her arm.

"I hear something. Shh. Arturo." Henry's eyes had adjusted to the dimness. "He's got an armful of food and he's shoving it into a garbage bag."

"He's stealing food from Coralee?" Emily accidentally bumped into a metal shelf, causing cans to fall off. She froze, knowing the sound would give them away.

"Who's here?" said Arturo. "What do you want?"

Henry whispered, "Let's run up the steps and get out of here."

She grabbed Henry's hand and her heart pounded. Did he know they were there?

When they got outside, she soon heard footsteps pounding behind them. Arturo was chasing them. She tried to drag Henry along, but he wasn't used to running the way she was. Arturo was gaining on them. Should they hide, or try to outrun him?

Pretty soon, it was obvious they'd have to hide or get caught. They ducked behind a tree. Emily frantically pulled pine needles over them.

"I know you're out here. I have a gun."

"A gun? Henry, what if he finds us?" She heard footsteps coming closer and closer. Her heart pounded like a jackhammer in her chest and she squeezed Henry's hand. She smelled Arturo's smoky breath as he came upon them.

"Found you!" Arturo's eyes went from one to the other.

Emily felt the blood drain from her face. "Don't hurt us. We have a daughter."

"Henry and Emily? What are you doing out here?"

Henry said, "Put the gun down, please Arturo. We won't harm you."

"Gun? What gun?"

"The one you said you had. The one you use to keep safe during your drug deals."

Arturo laughed. "Drug deals?"

Emily said, "We followed you down by the river. We saw you hand off money and a cardboard box."

"You think I'm dealing drugs? All Mexicans are drug dealers, right?"

"Then what were you doing there?" asked Henry.

"Come with me. Back to the cellar. I'll show you what's in the garbage bag I was about to bring down to the river."

Emily felt her fight or flight hormones kick in. If she ran, Arturo could only get either her or Henry. If he chased her, Henry could get back to the inn and call the police.

To Emily's surprise, Henry said, "Let's go. Lead the way." Why was he so trusting of Arturo? All along he didn't believe he was the killer. She still wasn't convinced.

Wondering with each step whether or not she should run the opposite way, she hoped Henry's instincts were correct. She put one foot in front of the other until they stood at the outside doors to the cellar.

"Follow me." Arturo started down the steps.

Emily whispered to Henry, "This isn't a good idea." Ignoring her request, Henry proceeded down the steps after Arturo and motioned her to follow him into the blackness.

"I'll show you what's in the bag," said Arturo. He flicked on the overhead light, stinging her eyes. He opened the bag. "Come on."

Henry reached in and pulled out a handful of its contents. "It's food. Cut up vegetables, bread, cheese."

"Those are the leftovers from dinner service. They'd go into the trash. I take them to the homeless community over by the river every night. Otherwise, those people would go hungry, especially in the winter. It's bad enough it's freezing and they have no medicine when they're sick."

"What about the money?"

"I give them a few dollars when I can. It's not much, but it buys blankets from the Goodwill store, and used clothing."

"Does Coralee know you're stealing from her?" said Emily.

"Stealing? Of course she does. You're friends with her, right? You know how caring she is."

Henry said, "I had a hard time buying you were a drug dealer, but you've got to admit it looked convincing."

Emily said, "So that's why you snuck out of the inn the night of the murder and returned an hour later. The police have you on CCTV. Why didn't you tell them you'd left that night instead of saying you were in your room all evening before going to the bar?"

"I didn't think they'd believe me, and I forgot about the surveillance cameras. Coralee gave me a pot of stew to bring that night. She'll vouch for me. And the police can question any one of the homeless people."

"Arturo, you're a good man."

"And you're most certainly not Faith Maguire's killer."

Chapter 17

The next morning, Emily went for a run around the lake. Arturo wasn't the killer, in fact, quite the opposite. He was helping those homeless people live. Back to the drawing board. She had a hunch about Rona. If she killed her own parents to get the house and turn it into a bed and breakfast, surely she had it in her to knock off Faith Maguire and cripple the competition. Then again, there was nothing definitively tying Rona to the inn the night of Faith's murder. The wet mulch on the galoshes set off a red flag in Emily's mind, but Megan said she checked Rona's alibi and she was at a friend's house, just as she claimed.

"Emily? I didn't know you ran." Jessica Pratt pulled her ponytail tighter.

"I do this route several mornings a week. I'm surprised we haven't run into each other before this."

"This is a new route for me. I generally stick to the roads, especially when the weather is bad. I do a few miles before work a couple of times a week."

"Speaking of work, I hear Mila Maguire is back at school. How's she doing?"

"Not as badly as you'd imagine. She talks a lot about her father. I think he's been a big comfort. Tilly, the housekeeper, has been keeping tabs. She emails me every night to see how Mila's day went."

"I'm glad she bonded with her father. Ava said Mila rarely got to spend time with him when they lived in Georgia. Has she had any more seizures?"

"She's only been back a few days. So far, she's been fine. How's Maddy?"

"Good. She's in the finals for the science fair. You should come to her school Friday night and see her project."

"She told me about it. Sam and I will be there."

"Sounds like you and Sam are a couple."

Jessica shrugged her shoulders. "Yeah, kinda. We've only been seeing each other a few weeks. Time will tell." She looked at her Garmin watch. "I'd better get going or I'll be late to school. I'll see you Friday. Tell Maddy I said hello."

"Will do." Emily shivered. Being sweaty, then standing still in the cold air was a sure way to get sick. Speaking of sick, she wondered how long it would be before she heard back from the breast center. They said a couple of days. Nonetheless, she'd continually checked her phone messages since the moment she left her appointment.

As she came around the bend, she spotted Kurt and Prancer. Like Maddy said, Kurt walked Prancer at certain times of the day like clockwork. Being regimented herself, it's no wonder she often ran into them during her morning runs.

"Morning, Emily."

She reached down to pet Prancer, who responded by licking her. "I'm a cat person, but boy has Prancer made me think about getting a dog. I just love him."

"Man's best friend. With Chloe away, he's the only family I've got."

"Why are you carrying a tool box?"

"Trent, the man who lives across the lake from us, has a rental cabin that needs a few repairs. I told him he could borrow my tools."

"Do you have a new tenant in Chloe's cabin yet?"

"Nah. This time of year it's hard to get renters. I'm hoping Chloe stays for the summer. Good thing I don't need the money like Trent does. He was lucky finding a tenant in the middle of winter but the guy already moved out."

"Kurt, do you know anything about cars?"

"I know how to drive them."

"Not what I meant. If someone had the right tools, could they learn how to cut the brakes or mess up the steering by watching a video on YouTube?"

"You what?"

"Never mind." I'd better get back. Take care, Kurt. Bye, Prancer my love." She kissed Prancer on the top of his head.

When she got back to their cabin, Henry and Maddy were eating breakfast.

"Maddy, I saw your sister by the lake this morning. I didn't know Jessica ran."

"I know she goes to the gym all the time."

"She said Mila seems to be doing okay at school. Her father has been a comfort."

"Yeah. He's only been here like a week but Ava's crazy about him and she said Mila clings to him and Tilly."

"Thank goodness those poor girls have people who love them and will help them through this."

"Was Sam with Jessica?"

"No, why?"

"She said he barely lets her out of his sight. They work together, and then he pops up at her house at random times like he's checking on her."

"Really? She said they'd only been together a few weeks."

"I know. That's why it's scary." She grabbed her backpack. "Gotta go. Bye Dad."

"Have a nice day."

After Emily heard the door close, she said, "I don't think she should be wearing those ripped jeans to school. The teachers are going to think we don't buy her clothes."

"I've seen her friends wear the same ripped jeans. I think it's the style. I'm proud of you for not hassling her about it."

"Like you said, you've got to pick your battles. I hope she wears one of the nice dresses I got her for Christmas to the science fair. The local paper will most likely be there taking pictures."

"I can see the headlines now. Daughter of Emily and Henry Fox shows up at science fair in ripped jeans. Hope they don't sic the Department of Child and Family Services on us."

"Very Funny."

"They'll be more interested in the projects than what the kids are wearing. You have to trust Maddy more."

Emily's phone vibrated. She jumped, as she did every time the phone rang since her appointment at the breast center.

"Who's calling you so early?"

She peeked at the screen. "It's my editor. She knows I'm an early riser."

"I've got to get going." He kissed her and grabbed his bag on the way out.

"Hello? So it's a go? Terrific. I'm already starting research on my next project. Thanks."

Yes! Now she could act on the urge to run with the Rona Smyth story. Convinced in her gut but cautious nevertheless, she had to assess the feasibility before investing a lot of time. How much did Rona know about cars and what were her movements in the days before the accident? How did she react to the news her parents were dead? Had she prepared ahead of time to open the inn—before she knew the house was soon to be hers? If she could prove Rona not only killed her parents but also Faith Maguire? That'd be a *New York Times* best seller for sure!

She poured another cup of coffee and settled down with her notes. She began sketching a timeline—Rona at cooking school, tampers with baking contest, Rona opens a restaurant, restaurant burns to the ground, Rona moves back home, Rona's parents die in suspicious auto accident, Rona turns family home into bed and breakfast…She jumped when the phone vibrated. Deep breath. She slowly turned over the phone to see the number. Not her doctor.

"Maddy? What's wrong? You're in school, right?"

"I forgot my permission slip for the science fair and it's due today."

"I signed that last week."

"But I left it home. Look on my desk or on the floor by my bed. Can you drop it off? Please?"

"Sure. I'll bring it to the front office."

Emily went to Maddy's room, where Chester was sleeping in the middle of the bed. She looked on the desk—graded assignments, an agenda, a paperback library book…No permission slip. She bent down and sorted through the pile on the floor next to the bed and easily located the permission slip. Before she stood up, Emily noticed something under Maddy's bed. She pulled out a stack of letter-sized envelopes held together with a hair tie.

Normally, she would have respected Maddy's privacy. This time, her daughter's safety had to come first. The return address? Chicago Penitentiary! She pulled out the first letter.

Dear Maddy,
I'm glad you didn't throw this out without reading it. I'm sure by now you've received word that I am your

biological father. I want you to know that though I've never met you, you are a part of me and the door is always open for you to write back or even visit....

Emily cringed. The nerve of this man! And why hadn't Maddy told them about this? There were several more letters in which he discussed his likes, dislikes, hobbies, medical history. She couldn't believe what she was reading. How could the prison allow these to be mailed? She would contact them immediately and put a stop to this.

She was about to leave the room, when she noticed something on Maddy's desk. It was an envelope addressed in Maddy's handwriting to her father at the prison. She felt herself turn pale. She looked at the notebook lying open on Maddy's desk. So far, she'd written and crossed out 'Dear Dr. Lipton' five times. Nothing else. Maddy was writing him back!

How was she supposed to handle this? She could Google *'how to stop your teenage daughter from writing to a convict.'* Right. It sounded like the subject of a Dr. Phil episode. Hmmm. Should she consult a therapist? She wanted to yell at Maddy and shake some sense into her. Knowing that was the wrong choice, she was glad she had time to digest it without Maddy being there. She called Henry and explained what she'd found.

"Em, I doubt she was intending to answer it without talking to us first. She must feel very confused. We should talk to Jessica and see if she's been getting letters."

"Good idea. I hadn't thought of that."

"Did you notice dates? How long has she been getting these letters?"

Emily sifted through the postmarks. "They've all been sent within the last few months."

"I'm going to talk to the police. He's harassing a minor."

"Can we get the prison to block him from sending these?"

"It worries me that he got our address in the first place. I'll see what the police say."

"Okay. I have to drop off Maddy's permission slip on my way to work. I'll see you tonight. Love you."

"Love you, too."

She ran a brush through her hair, dabbed on some lipstick, and headed to the school.

The school office had more security than Fort Knox. All she wanted to do was drop off the permission slip, but she found herself waiting behind another parent. The woman at the counter examined and copied down that parent's license number, had the parent sign a clipboard, took a photo, slapped on an ID badge...

While she waited, she saw Sam, huddled in a corner near the door, ear to his phone.

"Next. May I help you?"

"I just have to drop off this permission slip for my daughter."

"If they forget something at home, you're not supposed to bring it in. Otherwise, with no consequence, they don't learn responsibility."

She bit her tongue and calmly said, "It's for the science fair. If she doesn't turn it in today, she can't participate."

"The woman grumbled, then called into Maddy's classroom."

"Should I wait?"

"No. We'll get it to her. Next?"

Sam was still on his phone. If this school was anything like St. Edwards, phone service was spotty in places. She supposed that's why Sam had come up here to make his call. He whispered into the phone.

Wondering if Sam's secretive tone and guarded body language meant he was cheating on Jessica, she stood still behind one of the artificial trees flanking the office door.

"Yeah, the obstacle has been eradicated. We can move forward. I can add to my initial investment only if you can guarantee it'll be operational in time for the next school year. I've got another potential investor on the hook. Okay, then." Sam tucked the phone into his pocket just as the bell rang.

*****

Henry hadn't sat down all morning. He was about to go to lunch, when the EMTs rushed in with a man whose hand was bleeding through the gauze it'd been wrapped in.

"What happened here?"

"Man was doing repairs on his rental cabin and the saw slipped. He'll be lucky if he doesn't lose that hand. People shouldn't try these do-it-yourself fixes when they don't know what they're doing. Spend the few bucks and stay safe. It should be a public service announcement."

"You know I'm not unconscious and can hear what you're saying, right?" said the man on the stretcher. "You think I'm gonna lose my hand?"

Henry said, "Let's not panic. Let me get a look at it."

The EMT helped Henry get the man settled in a cubicle before leaving. Henry looked at his patient and said, "What's your name?"

"Trent Adams."

"Tell me what happened, Trent?"

"I had a tenant who just moved out. Guy was there only one month. He lost his deposit, but still I depend on the rent to get by. I got a lead on someone wanting to see the place this weekend and had to get over there and repair a few things."

"With a saw?"

"The door frame had rotted out in spots so I was making a replacement."

Henry examined and cleaned the wound. "We'll get some films and I'll call in a consult. At first glance, looks like you'll just need some stitches. Are you up to date on your tetanus shot?"

"Yeah. Had to get one last year when I put that nail through my finger. Thanks, Doc."

A nurse called Henry over. "We have a little girl who's been vomiting. She has a history of seizures. The father's with her."

Henry recognized Mila right away. "Hi, Mila. Do you remember me?"

"We ate dinner with you the night my...the night Mommy died."

"That's right. I'm going to help you feel better. Tell me what hurts. Your tummy? Your head?"

"I don't know. Everything."

Henry turned to the father. "When did this start?"

"We'd just eaten breakfast and I was about to drop her off at school when she said she didn't feel well and ran into the bathroom."

"How many times has she vomited?"

"Just that once, but she says she feels like it's going to happen again. She gets seizures."

"What are these seizures like? Do they start with vomiting?"

"I don't know. I shared custody with her mother but more often than not there was some reason I couldn't see her. The past few months, I haven't seen her at all. My wife trumped up false accusations and the court rescinded my visitation rights."

"Mila, do you feel like this before you get your seizures?"

"No."

"What did you eat for breakfast?"

"I ate some cereal, but then my tummy started hurting."

"It hurt after you ate the cereal?"

"It started hurting when I woke up and got dressed for school."

Henry said, "Is it hard going to school since your Mommy died?"

Mila started crying.

Dave Maguire hugged her. "It's okay, honey. You don't have to go to school if you're not ready yet."

After Mila's sobs subsided, Henry said, "How many times did you throw up?"

"Well, I didn't throw up. I felt like I was going to throw up."

"That's not what you told me," said Dave Maguire. He turned to Henry. "She said she threw up and I was worried with her history and all."

"Your wife said she had problems with dairy. Maybe the milk in the cereal…"

"Problems with dairy? The girl guzzles a bowl of ice cream every night for dessert and I haven't seen any issues. Mila, do you get sick when we eat ice cream?"

"No, Daddy."

Henry said, "Mila, do you still feel sick, or do you think thinking about school made your tummy hurt?"

Mila didn't answer.

"Mila, answer the doctor. He's trying to help you."

"I wanted to stay with my Daddy. I didn't want him to go away like Mommy did."

"Doctor, I'm sorry we wasted your time."

"Absolutely no problem. She's going through a lot. You all are. With her medical history, you were smart to bring her in."

"Thanks. I appreciate it. It's scary suddenly being a full time father again."

"I know. You always wonder if you're doing the right thing or if there's a better way. I've got a daughter. She's friends with Ava as a matter of fact."

"Maddy Fox. Now I put it together. She kind of looks like you."

Henry didn't bother explaining she wasn't his biological child. Instead, he just smiled. "Call if she feels worse, but I'm going to prescribe sipping soup and watching TV all afternoon with her Daddy. The nurse will be in shortly with paperwork."

Henry went out to the nurse's station to write up his notes and return a few phone calls. Trent, the man who'd injured his hand with the saw, was wheeled by on his way to radiology. He asked the orderly to stop for a moment.

"Doc, this is already starting to hurt. Should I take some Aleve?"

"I'll write you a prescription for something a little stronger." He took out his prescription pad. As he wrote it out, Dave Maguire and Mila passed them.

"Thanks again, Dr. Fox."

Trent, who was facing away waiting for the prescription, turned his head. "Doc, that's the guy."

"What guy?"

"My tenant. The one who was only there for a month. I figured he'd left town by now."

"Are you sure? His wife was killed. I'm sure you saw it on the news. He got into town last week to take care of his daughters."

"No, I'm sure it's him. He's a Braves fan. From Atlanta, right?"

He *was* wearing a Braves shirt under his coat. Henry couldn't make sense of it. Dave Maguire flew in the night the Southeast had that terrible blizzard. He couldn't have been renting Trent's cabin for the past month, could he?

Chapter 18

Henry rolled over and looked at the clock by his bed. 5 a.m. He couldn't sleep thinking about Maddy writing to a prisoner and to a lesser extent, Dave Maguire lying about when he got to town. He felt Emily tossing and turning all night as well.

"Em, are you awake?" He whispered in her ear.

She rolled over, hugging the quilt. "Yeah. I didn't sleep at all. I keep picturing Maddy visiting her father in prison. What if she wants to meet him?" She omitted her worry over the test results she was expecting. "I'm going to try to reach Jessica before she leaves for work."

"Can you imagine finding out your father is a felon? I'm sure Fiona thought the sperm donor was a good Samaritan trying to help a couple have a baby. What an egomaniac, fathering all those kids. Not to mention the horrible breech of professional ethics."

"Poor Fiona must be rolling over in her grave. I almost wish Jessica never found out about him."

"I suppose the medical history might prove useful someday."

"I think when you use a sperm donor you get that information, but I could be wrong."

"Speaking of fathers, what do you make of Dave Maguire lying about when he got to town?"

"Are you sure that patient of yours wasn't mistaken?" Then she remembered her conversation with Kurt yesterday morning. "Although, Kurt told me he lent his toolbox to a friend who had found a short term renter."

"Trent? Was that the friend? Lives across the lake?"

"As a matter of fact, it was."

"Let's examine this logically. Whether or not it's true, Faith Maguire accuses Dave of abusing the girls. She gets the court to give her full custody, so now she can move out of state and accept a high-paying job as a school superintendent."

"Maybe he did abuse them. What about those seizures Mila gets?"

"Dave claims he's never witnessed one. If I were in his shoes, I'd have tried to keep in touch with my daughter. I can't imagine if you took Maddy away somewhere and I couldn't see her. I'd go to any length."

"So he sneaks into Sugarbury Falls and rents a cabin from Kurt's friend. After Faith dies, he moves into the house with Tilly and the girls. Did he plan to murder Faith all along, or did she figure out he was in town?"

"The girls must have known he was here, don't you think?"

"Maybe not. I'm not sure I'd trust a seven-year-old not to let that sort of information leak to Mommy."

"Then what's the point of moving here if he wasn't visiting with the girls?"

"Being close by, watching...better than being all the way in Georgia."

Emily checked her phone both for the time and the weather report. Convinced it was warm enough to brave the outdoors at this hour, she got up and pulled on leggings and a long-sleeved running top.

"Going for a run? I thought you wanted to catch Jessica before she left for work."

"I was hoping I might run into her again outside. Besides, it's still too early to call her." She stretched her auburn hair into a barely-there ponytail. "I won't be long."

A sky full of stars and a full moon broke up the blackness of the late winter sky. The crisp air stung her cheeks. She pulled down her ski cap, fastened on her runner's headlamp, and turned on her music before heading out. She did her best thinking when she ran. Being it was earlier than when she normally ran, the path was deserted.

When she reached the lake, she felt the ground vibrate. Taking out her ear buds, she heard the sound of a motor...no, a motorcycle. By the time she turned around, it whizzed right past her. Her heart skipped a beat. After she recovered her breath, she chastised herself for leaving her phone on the nightstand. She listened. She looked in all directions. Confident the danger had passed; she began jogging once again.

Even with her earbuds in place, she heard it before she saw it. Sounded like a lawn mower. Then the headlights. Blinding. The motorcycle had done an about face and headed straight at her! Fight or flight. She felt the hormones surge. Fighting a speeding motorcycle? Not a feasible option. At the last second, she jumped aside, narrowly dodging it—for a moment.

It once again circled back, headlights like evil eyes burning through her. In the moonlight, she could only see the driver wore a black, leather jacket and helmet with a tinted face shield. There was no telling who it was, even if it was a man or a woman. Even with the piercing headlights.

Like an angry bee, it buzzed toward her again, determined to sting its target. Her mind raced through the choices. Stand and get run over. Run, and make it a little tougher for the driver, then get run over. Or... The lake. Not a first choice, but a desperate one. She jumped, feet first into the icy water.

Freezing cold water rushed up her nose as she plunged beneath the surface. Her ear buds popped out and the water fled into her ears. When she emerged, she heard the muffled sound of a waning motorcycle.

The sun was just beginning to show itself as she swam to the shore, shivering. Exhausted but fueled by adrenaline, she clawed her way up the river bank. Now what? She gave herself a moment to get her breathing under control, then made her way to the path.

Barking, yipping...Prancer! He dragged Kurt behind him as he ran to her.

"Emily! What happened?"

"It was..." Her teeth chattered as she spoke. "A motorcycle chased me. I had no choice. I jumped into the lake." She rubbed her ear trying to clear the pressure and stop her voice from echoing inside her head.

Kurt took off his thin, nylon jacket and put it around her. "On purpose?"

"Of course. It circled back when it missed the first time."

"Did you see who it was?"

"No. Couldn't even tell whether it was a man or a woman. You didn't hear a motorcycle?"

"No."

"Then it came from the other direction. Away from our cabins. Toward the exit from town."

"Does this have to do with a mystery you're chasing? Faith Maguire's murder, perhaps?"

"Possibly."

"Let's get you home. Henry must be worried by now." He put his arm around her and walked her home. He was right. Henry had been worried.

"Emily, what happened? You're soaking wet!"

"I was chased into the lake by a motorcycle. Prancer found me and Kurt helped me home. I'm freezing."

"Thanks, Kurt." He scratched Prancer between the ears, "You too, buddy."

"I'm going to take a hot shower and put on dry clothes. Where's Maddy?"

"She already left for school." He followed her up the ladder to their loft and talked to her through the shower door. "Someone doesn't want you to find Faith's murderer."

"Or to pursue Rona Smyth's past." The steam filled her lungs and the warmth soothed her body.

"Why don't you heed the warning and find another story. There are tons of crimes out there to write about."

"Ah, but if someone is chasing me away, it means I'm on to a juicy one."

"After your shower, let's go to the station and report this. You have a family to think of. You can't make selfish decisions."

"Selfish? You're kidding, right?"

"You know what I mean. Is a story worth leaving Maddy without a mother? Again?"

She ran her soapy hand over her breast and remembered how worried she was about that very issue.

"You're right. I'm not going to do anything foolish."

"Good."

"I have an idea. After we go to the station, let's do something fun together. We could have a late lunch, maybe a picnic by the water."

"It's too cold for a picnic."

"Not if we take blankets. I can make a Thermos full of hot chocolate and we can get soup to go from Coralee."

"If we stop at the inn, you'll be gabbing with Coralee and it'll be hard to break away."

"How about from Smyth Haven?"

"You're kidding, right?"

"It's on the way out of town. We can take our lunch over to the covered bridge. Remember how we took the Hibachi over there and had dinner. Before Maddy came to live with us."

"And we got eaten by mosquitos so we took off our clothes and jumped into the river for a swim? Yeah, I remember, but it was the middle of July."

"The fireflies. Remember the fireflies?"

Henry smiled. "Of course. And then we ate the brownies. Go make the hot chocolate."

With a picnic basket full of sandwiches, hot cocoa, and a bag of baked potato chips in the back of the Jeep, they stopped at the police station. Megan greeted them at the counter.

"You said on the phone that you heard a motorcycle but couldn't identify the rider, correct?"

"It was dark and he wore black."

"I sent an officer to the scene. He took an impression of motorcycle tracks leading away from the path and toward the river. He spoke to the owner of the nearest cabin, but he'd been asleep at the time and didn't see anything. Are you sure no one else was out there? An early morning speed walker? The newspaper delivery boy?"

"No, it was deserted except for the two of us. Did you see if Rona Smyth had an alibi?"

"You mentioned her on the phone. We'll check the security footage. Meanwhile, be careful. Use the treadmill for now."

Henry and Emily got back in the jeep. Henry said, "Next stop Smyth Haven. Are you sure it's the soup you want?"

"What do you mean?"

"You're not going to try to question Rona Smyth after what Megan just said."

"Of course not. I just want soup to bring on our picnic."

"I was thinking we should be honest with Maddy about the letters you found. I'll explain how dangerous it could be to get into a corresponding relationship with a nut job."

"The nut job is her father."

"I'm her father."

"Of course you are. I meant, she may be overly sensitive because she shares half her genes with this man. What if she's worried she's inherited his criminal gene?"

"I can show her all sorts of research saying nurture rules over nature."

"What if she says she wants to meet him?"

"We're her parents. The answer is no. When she becomes a legal adult she can do as she pleases, but at the moment she has to play by our rules."

"That sounds reasonable. I'll try to enlist Jessica's help in dissuading her."

They pulled in front of Smyth Haven. "They need better parking," said Henry. "The lot is full."

"You can park around the back."

They walked into Smyth Haven through the back door and caught Rona hugging a young man. Emily whispered, "He must be half her age!"

Before she turned around, Rona said to the young man, "I love you. See you tonight. Thanks for having my back." She jumped when she noticed Henry and Emily in the doorway.

"Can I help you?"

Emily said, "I was here the other day and the pastry was delicious. We're going on a picnic and I wanted to grab some soup to go. Is it possible?"

Rona smiled. "Of course. We just started lunch service. I made a big batch of clam chowder."

Emily said, "I'm vegetarian. Any other choices?"

"I have tomato soup in the fridge from last night. I'll heat it up for you."

"Great."

While they waited for the soup, Emily said, "I wonder how long she's been involved with the jail bait. Maybe he helped her murder her parents or poison the cheesecake."

"That's a leap. Besides, I thought the point of this afternoon was to relax and forget our problems."

"Of course, you're right. Coralee's place feels, I don't know, happier."

"Rona should have chosen a brighter wall paper or used white trim. It's too dark in here."

"Shh. Here comes Rona."

Henry handed Rona his credit card while Emily took the Styrofoam container from Rona.

"Enjoy. Come back for dinner one night. After you taste the soup, you'll be back for more."

"Finally on our way," said Henry. He opened the passenger door for Emily.

"Henry, look! It's a motorcycle leaving the parking lot!"

"Rona couldn't have run out here without us seeing her."

"Do you think it was her boyfriend?"

"Maybe. He'd have no reason to come after you."

"Of course he has a reason. Rona told him I'm getting nosy and he's protecting her!"

"You know what? We were planning a nice, romantic lunch weren't we?"

"You're right. The sleuthing can wait. I'll call Megan after we get home."

Henry drove out to the river by the covered bridge. The sky was the color of a Robin's egg, clear with just a few swirls of clouds. "This is our spot, right?"

"Yep. We ate under that big oak tree. Looks different without its leaves, but that's it all right. Come on."

Henry took the basket; Emily bundled up the blankets. "We can lay out the blanket here. Put down the basket and give me a hand."

They smoothed out the blanket, then wrapped another around them. Emily opened the Thermos and poured hot cocoa into two thick cups. "Want egg salad, or cheese?"

"Either is fine." He opened the lid of the soup. "This smells terrific." He took a sip. "I hate to say it, but Rona gives Coralee a run for her money in the soup department."

Emily cuddled next to Henry. After all these years, she tingled when they touched. His hands felt muscular, yet soft when he held hers. His soft eyes with the crinkles around them when he smiled made her melt like they did the first time they met.

"More soup?"

"Sure. It's so peaceful out here. In the summer there are visitors all over that bridge."

"Are you cold?"

"Nope. You should suggest this place to Pat. It'd be a memorable place to pop the question."

"I'll suggest it. Are you happy we moved here when we inherited the cabin? Do you ever miss New York?"

"I haven't once doubted we made the right move. I don't miss being called to crime scenes at all hours of the night, or you working holidays. How about you?"

"Not at all. I'm glad I decided to help out the hospital part time. I feel, I don't know, needed I guess is the word."

"And teaching a few classes and writing my books? I have time to run and make healthy meals. It's the perfect balance."

Henry pulled her closer and she felt his soft lips on hers. "I love you more every day."

"Stop talking." He continued kissing her, making her feel like they were a teenage couple at Lover's Lane. She felt peaceful and loved. And lucky. Very lucky.

Chapter 19

"Come on, Maddy. We don't want to be late," said Emily. "Parking in that small lot with all those parents will be a bear if we don't hurry."

Maddy screamed, "I'm coming!" She slammed the door to her room.

When she'd changed from an ogre back into to a princess, Henry said, "You look beautiful. Blue's a good color for you. It matches your science board, right?"

Maddy's face softened. "Since when are bean plants blue?"

"They might be, if your hypothesis wasn't supported. If you feed bean plants coffee grinds, then they won't turn blue. No wonder you're a finalist!"

"Very funny, Dad. Just don't say stuff like that around my teachers or my friends...or my friends' parents, okay?"

"When shouldn't I say it? Before or after I reveal my *Father of a Scientist* t-shirt? I'm wearing it under my sweater." He tugged at the collar of his undershirt.

Emily, feeling too stressed about getting there on time to be amused, said, "Have you got everything? We have to go."

"I've got my notecards and my purse. I'm set." She took one last look in the mirror and stuck her phone back in her purse.

As Emily predicted, the small lot in front of the school was nearly full when they arrived. They headed to the cafeteria, where projects were displayed on rows of tables at the stage end of the barn-like room. Maddy took her place next to her board, notecards in hand. Ava's project was right next to Maddy's.

Emily whispered to Henry, "Poor Ava. I'm sure she wishes her mother was here to see this."

"I'm glad the projects were due well before Faith was killed. There's Dave Maguire with Mila and the housekeeper. What's her name again?"

"Tilly."

Henry walked over to Ava's project. "So, how much would it cost to swap out the eight windows in my cabin for these blizzard proof windows?"

Ava, sounding like a scientist, answered, "It depends on the size of your windows, but you have to figure in the savings on your heating bill as well, as these insulate twice as well as traditional glass windows."

Henry said, "We should have tried this out. We just had to replace a window."

Ava answered, "These windows don't actually exist. It's just a project."

Dave Maguire, who'd been within earshot, replied, "Yet. They don't exist yet, but I think she's onto something."

"Dad, if it wasn't for you I never would have come up with this material, let alone been able to make and cut it to fit the model like you did." Turned our barn into a woodshop. You should stop over one day.

Mila, clinging to Tilly, said, "Daddy made me a dollhouse and he put blizzard proof windows in there for me."

"Your Daddy's handy with building." He turned to Dave, "I do woodworking myself. We turned our barn into a woodshop. You should stop over one day."

"I'd like that."

Emily said, "There's Jessica. I'll be right back."

Jessica, with Sam at her side, was making her way through the rows of projects. Emily said, "Jessica, can I talk to you for a moment? In private?"

Sam gave her a look. "You can talk in front of me."

"This is private, family business. We'll only be a moment." She led Jessica to a corner of the cafeteria.

"Emily, is something wrong? Is Maddy okay?"

"I'm just going to spit it out. Has your biological father been in touch with you?"

"You mean super sperm? No. He's in jail. How would he even know I exist?"

"Well, somehow he knows about Maddy. He wrote to her from prison. Maddy has a stack of letters under her bed from him."

"You've got to be kidding. What did Maddy say about it?"

"I haven't confronted her yet. The worst part is, she was working on a reply. I don't want her having contact with him."

"I don't blame you! I can't figure out how he found her, or why the prison allowed him to send her letters. You have to tell her to stay clear. Maybe you can get some sort of restraining order."

"We intend to put a stop to this. Will you back us up? I'm expecting resistance from Maddy."

"Of course. Let me know when you've talked to her and I'll follow up."

Sam strutted up to them. "Jessica, are you done?"

Jessica shook her head. "I told you to give me a minute."

"It's okay," said Emily. "I should be getting back to Maddy. Come see her project."

"That's why we're here."

"And thanks for supporting us."

"Of course."

As Emily started back, she heard Sam question Jessica. "What was that all about? Support them how?" She didn't like his tone or his body language. She was about to chase after them and say something about treating women with respect when she noticed a business card had fallen out of his pocket. She picked it up. *Fielding Construction.* Henry waved to her. "I'll be right there." She worked her way back to Maddy's project.

Dave Maguire was browsing through the displays. "Look at how clever these kids are. One of them will cure cancer someday."

Emily certainly hoped that day would come sooner rather than later.

"And did you see this? It's a device you stick into food and it reads how many carbs it has and the insulin you'd need to cover it. What a help for diabetics. My own mother could sure use that. Every time I take her out to a restaurant, she frets about whether she's getting the right amount of insulin because it's hard to figure what's in some of those restaurant dishes."

Henry came around the corner. "You have to see this, both of you." He led them down the row to where Maddy and Ava were. "Look. Both Maddy and Ava are going on to the state competition. Isn't that something?"

Emily noticed the blue ribbons stuck to the two boards. "Wow! I'm so proud of both of you."

Dave hugged his daughter. "I knew you had a winner there."

Ava said, "I wish Mom was here to see this."

"I'm sorry she isn't," said Dave. "However, if she was alive, I wouldn't have been allowed to be a part of this and I wouldn't want to have missed this for the world."

Emily said, "I'm sure your Mom knows and is smiling up in heaven. Maddy's mom is doing the same."

The principal took the microphone and when the feedback was under control, announced the three finalists who would be moving on to the state level. She handed each a certificate. Emily took out her phone and must have clicked a dozen pictures of Maddy as well as a few of Ava—in case her dad was too new at this sort of thing to think of it. The principal invited everyone to have punch and cookies, courtesy of the PTA.

Maddy said, "Can we skip the cookies? I'm tired. Can we go home now?"

"Sure. Come on." Henry said, "Do you have your certificate?"

"Yes, it's right here."

"We'll have to buy a nice frame for it," said Emily.

"I've got a better idea. I'll make one in my woodworking shop and we can customize it with the date. I'll paint it blue so it doesn't match the bean plants."

"Funny, Dad."

Henry had barely started the Jeep when he saw in the rearview mirror that Maddy had fallen asleep in the back.

"Emily, did you notice what Ava said? She said her father helped her with the project."

"I'm sure she was able to call him or *Facetime*, even if Faith didn't know about it."

"But he cut the windows for her. He'd have to be here in the flesh to do that. The projects were due weeks ago, right?"

"Last month. You're right."

"And he put the windows in Mila's playhouse, too. When, since Faith's death, did he have the time to do that?"

"Mila was playing with a home-made dollhouse when we dropped food by right after Faith's death."

"I think Dave Maguire has been in town for over a month. He rented Trent's cabin, then when Faith was killed, he moved into the house. Trent identified him at the hospital earlier. Remember the snow storm in Atlanta? He couldn't have gotten here when he said he did."

"You're right. Mila seemed awfully comfortable with him, considering she'd barely ever visited with him and Faith had gotten full custody. You think he snuck into town and killed Faith so he could be with his daughters?"

"He lied, almost certainly, and now his alibi about being in Georgia is blown out of the water. The police have to find out where he really was the night it happened. If I was forbidden from seeing my child…just saying."

"In other words, he had motive."

"A strong one."

Chapter 20

Saturday meant a leisurely breakfast for Emily and Henry, and extra hours of sleep for Maddy. Emily poured food into Chester's bowl and sat down at the table with a copy of the crossword puzzle.

Henry said, "We should call Megan and tell her what we figured out about Dave Maguire."

"How about if we verify the dates with Trent first? Wasn't Pat taking her on that picnic today? To propose?"

"You're right."

"By the way, I spoke to Jessica last night at the science fair and she said she would talk to Maddy about staying clear of her inmate father. We should talk to her before that, but I hate admitting I was snooping."

"You weren't snooping. You had a reason for being in her room."

"It was her fault. If she hadn't forgotten her permission slip…"

"Look, what's considered snooping under normal circumstances is just plain parenting when it involves a teenager. One of the nurses at the hospital has all her daughter's passwords and regularly checks her social media accounts. You can't be too careful these days. Remember a few months ago—the girl who was lured out of her house in the middle of the night by a predator? If her parents had kept a closer eye…"

Emily shuddered. "You're right." She popped a bagel in the toaster.

Henry looked out the window. "It's awfully cloudy. I hope the weather holds up for Pat and Megan's big picnic."

Maddy came into the kitchen. "What big picnic?"

Henry said, "You have to swear to secrecy?"

Maddy played along. "Yes, Dad." She raised her right hand. "I, Maddy Fox, swear to keep the secret my father is about to tell me at all costs."

Emily said, "This is important."

"Pat is going to propose to Megan. He planned a picnic by the lake this afternoon."

"Isn't it a little cold for a picnic?"

Henry smiled at Emily. "It can be done."

Emily said, "We'll have to plan a nice engagement party at the inn."

Henry said, "You're assuming she'll say yes." He looked at Emily and Maddy's faces. "Just kidding. Of course she'll say yes."

Emily said, "Come, sit down. We have to talk to you."

"Uh-oh." She rolled her eyes. "What now?"

"When you asked me to fetch your permission slip the other day, I found the letters under your bed. The ones from your biological father." She watched Maddy's face turn red.

"You spied on me!"

Henry intercepted, "Don't go getting all indignant. We're your parents and it's our job to keep you safe. Why didn't you tell us you'd been getting mail from him?"

"Because I knew you'd be like this."

"Like what?" Emily took the bait.

"Like I'm not supposed to care about my real parents."

"That's so unfair I can't believe those words just came out of your mouth."

"Why? Because my real mother made you my guardian, despite your preference not to have your own kids? Because you felt obligated? Because I tried to kill myself?"

Henry said, "We've done nothing but love and protect you as if you were our own, but we never tried to take Fiona's place."

"Emily never talks about her." She looked at Emily. "Do you even remember her? You were friends in college. Before she died, when was the last time you spoke to her?"

"That's not fair. We may have lost touch, but..."

Henry said, "This isn't about your mother, it's about your biological father. Fiona never meant for him to be in your life. He was supposed to be an anonymous donor."

"And it turns out he's a felon," said Emily. "I'm sure if your friend Brooke was in the same situation Nancy wouldn't let her visit him in jail."

"What does Brooke have to do with this? She knows her father. You aren't even making sense."

"We just want to keep you safe. If you need more information about his medical history, we can get that for you."

"Medical history? I want to know where I got my big feet, or my crooked smile, or my love of science. Those didn't come from my mother."

"You have Jessica. And I'll bet you'll find other half siblings if you're curious about your genes," said Emily.

"I hate you," said Maddy. She stormed out of the kitchen.

Henry said, "Wait for it...there."

The door slammed shut, shaking the floor. "I make her feel like I don't care about Fiona?"

"That's nonsense. She's just striking out. She isn't fully in control of her emotions. Her frontal lobe isn't developed yet."

"Fiona should have chosen someone more capable. Maybe someone who had experience raising a biological child."

"That's nonsense. No more pity party. Go get dressed and let's take a walk over to Trent's place."

By the time they were ready to go out, it was late morning. They walked around the lake to Trent's cabin and found him outside stacking firewood.

"Hey, Doc. Making a house call? I changed the bandages like you told me, see?"

"I always appreciate it when my patients follow directions."

"Can I help you with something?"

Henry said, "I was wondering if you can tell us more about Dave Maguire, the one you saw at the hospital the other day."

"The short term renter? I barely know him."

"When did he start his lease?"

"Must have been beginning of February. Only stayed a month."

"Was he planning on staying longer?"

"He'd signed a three-month lease. I didn't hold him to it when he told me what happened to his ex-wife and all."

"Did he rent the place and fly back and forth?"

"No. Once he moved in he was here."

Emily said, "Did you ever see him with his daughters? Did he bring them here?"

"Yeah. He had a girl around, I don't know, 12, 13 years old. He was helping her build model houses. Had this fan blowing packing peanuts. Made a mess out of the yard but he cleaned it up before he moved out."

"Thanks, Trent. Take care of that hand, now."

Henry said, "Em, we have to tell the police."

"Isn't Pat proposing to Megan today?"

"Then we should tell Ron. Dave Maguire lied and had a good reason for wanting Faith dead. I wonder if he has an alibi? We never told the police we spotted the motorcycle at Smyth Haven either."

"What alibi? No one knew he was here." Emily felt a chill. The sky was gray and snow flurries fell onto her jacket, melting into specks of water when they made contact. She picked up the pace.

Henry hurried to keep up with her. "My phone is buzzing. It's Maddy."

"At least she's still speaking to you."

"Maddy? Yeah, okay. We're almost home. I'll drop you off when we get there."

Emily said, "Drop her off where?"

"Ava's. She's going to help Ava catch up on the schoolwork she missed."

"I'll come with you. We can stop by the police station afterwards."

Maddy was waiting, backpack in hand when they opened the front door.

"Why do you both have to come?"

"We have somewhere to go afterwards. If you'd prefer to walk…"

"It's fine." She climbed into the back of the Jeep and stuck her earbuds into her ears. When they arrived at Ava's, Henry said, "Let's go in with her. We can have a chat with Dave Maguire if he's home."

Tilly answered the door. "Come on in, Ava. Henry and Emily, right? Come in before you get wet. The snow is picking up. One day you think it's just about spring and the next? They're predicting several inches between now and the morning."

Dave came into the foyer holding Mila. "Thanks for bringing Maddy by. Ava's having a hard time catching up, especially with geometry. You miss a few days in a class like that and suddenly it all looks Greek. Never was much of a math person myself."

"Maddy's a natural born teacher. Glad she can help," said Henry. "Dave, do you have a minute? Emily and I would like to talk to you." He looked at Mila, clinging to his neck. "Alone, if that's possible."

"I'll take her," said Tilly. "Come here, my little love. Do you want to help me make those cookies we talked about?" She took Mila into the kitchen.

"Come, sit down. What do you want to talk about?"

Henry said, "I don't know how to bring this up tactfully. You said you got to town the evening Faith's body was found."

"That's right."

"But there was a blizzard going on, and all the flights were canceled or delayed. You said you flew through Atlanta."

Dave looked at the floor. "That's right. I got lucky. Found a seat on the last plane out."

"I also know that you were renting a cabin for at least a month prior to when you said you flew here."

"I, um, I rented it so I'd have it for spring break—so I could visit with the girls. Flew out, rented it, went back to Savannah."

Emily said, "I thought Faith had taken out a restraining order?"

Henry added, "And I know you helped Ava with her science project. Your landlord verified it."

"It wasn't a restraining order. Okay. So I missed my girls. A lot. Ava had been secretly texting me and was desperate to see me. She said Mila missed me, too. And Mila was ill. I thought the stress of being away from me may have been a contributing factor."

Henry said, "But you were violating the law. Why didn't you just appeal the court decision?"

"I was saving money to do just that. Attorneys don't come cheap, you know. And I needed a more skilled one than I'd gotten the first time."

Emily blurted out, "Did you kill your wife?"

"What? No. Of course not. I could never…"

"Do you have an alibi? For the night she was killed?"

"Yes, um…I do but I can't say."

"What do you mean you can't say?" said Henry. "If you don't provide an alibi, the police are going to charge you with murder." He knew the police needed more than suspicion to arrest him but hoped Dave would fall for his bluff.

"You have nothing tying me to the scene. No physical evidence, no eyewitness statements. Besides, where would I get that drug that killed her?"

"You said your mother was diabetic, the night of the science fair."

"And my mother lives in Savannah. Do you think I grabbed some of her meds, stuck them in my suitcase, then spiked Faith's dessert with them? Get real. Those drugs are prescription. You can't just take them away from someone who depends on it."

"Then why don't you tell us where you were that night?"

"It's embarrassing."

"I don't think we have a brothel or a casino in town, so how bad could it be?"

"I was…don't hold this against me."

"Go on," said Henry.

"I'm an alcoholic. Have been most of my adult life. That's why my marriage didn't last. After Faith threw me out, I hit rock bottom. A friend from work helped me—brought me to my first AA meeting. I haven't had a drink since, I swear."

"So you were at a bar the night Faith was killed?" asked Emily. Clearly she wasn't getting it.

"No! I was at an AA meeting in the basement of St. Mary's church."

"Will anyone vouch for you?"

"Yeah. My new sponsor was there and half a dozen others."

"Well, you shouldn't be ashamed. You're getting help for a disease. Takes a big man to admit he needs help." Henry gave him a fist bump.

"You won't tell Ava will you?"

"Of course not."

"Thanks. It's actually a relief to get that off my chest. I just want to be a good dad for my girls."

Emily said, "I'm so sorry. We thought…If you need anything, help with the girls, anything—you can count on us."

At home, Emily changed into sweat pants and furry socks, then snuggled on the sofa next to Henry.

Henry said, "That was embarrassing. We sure got that wrong."

"I know, but I'm glad we found out Dave is innocent. Imagine if those poor girls had to have their father locked up in jail?" She suddenly remembered the father in jail scenario in relation to Maddy.

Henry's phone buzzed. "Hey, buddy. So when's the wedding?"

"Your guess is as good as mine."

"What happened? She didn't say no did she?"

"I never got to ask. The winter picnic idea was a disaster. It started snowing, the food got wet, our clothes got soaked…"

"You could have turned that around."

"Yeah, right. It's back to the drawing board."

Chapter 21

"Come on, Maddy. Jessica and Sam are waiting for us and you know how hard it is to get a table for Sunday brunch at the inn."

Maddy said, "You don't have to yell. I'm ready. Where's Dad?"

"Warming up the car."

When they arrived at the inn, Emily was glad to see Sunday brunch was as busy as ever and hoped Coralee felt reassured that the murder wasn't going to permanently harm her business. Jessica and Sam had already gotten a table and waved them over.

Jessica said, "Maddy, I'm so proud of you for going on to the state science fair. When is it?"

"Not until May."

Sam said, "Where do you have to go?"

"Burlington. We get to stay overnight in a fancy hotel."

"Too bad the school doesn't pick up the cost," said Henry. "Not that we mind. It's quite an honor."

"Public schools have their flaws, that's for sure," said Sam. "Where does all that tax money go? Certainly not to our salaries, and facilities? The roof in my classroom leaks every time it rains or snows. You'd think with the computers in there they'd want to get it fixed."

Summer Martin brought menus to the table. She acted like she didn't at all remember the scene she'd made when they were here with Faith and the girls. Emily guessed she'd been so focused on Faith she really didn't notice who else was at the table. Otherwise, she'd be embarrassed. If she was in Summer's shoes, *she'd* feel embarrassed.

"Coffee?"

"Yes, please. What are the specials?" asked Emily.

"Blueberry pancakes with sour cream compote, and a spicy sausage and cheddar omelet. I'll be back in a minute to take your orders."

Henry said, "Have you had Coralee's blueberry pancakes? They're second only to her blueberry French toast."

Jessica said, "Isn't it hard to find blueberries this time of year?"

"We think she has a secret garden in the basement," said Henry.

"I'll go with the pancakes," said Jessica.

"The spicy omelet sounds good to me," said Sam.

Emily closed her menu. "Sam, how are you liking Sugarbury Falls?"

"It's a nice change of pace."

"It's a special place. We love it here. Have you always been in education?"

"No, I switched to teaching recently. I was in investment banking. When the stock market took a dive, I changed fields—saw the handwriting on the wall."

"You know, everyone and his brother thinks they can be a teacher. When people lose their jobs, the first thing they think of is teaching, right? We learned that in college. There's no mystique to teaching. Not everyone thinks they can be a plumber or a dentist, but everyone can teach."

"Excuse me," said Sam.

"Oh, I didn't mean you. You have expertise in your field and you've made the adjustment well."

"I like to think so," said Sam.

Jessica said, "I got a new match on *Ancestors Are Us*. Maddy, we have a half-brother in New York. I wrote to him. His name is Jeff and he's in his thirties."

"In his thirties? Dr. Lipton got away with this for some time." Emily sipped her coffee.

"More than two decades, believe it or not. Had it not been for all the commercial DNA kits, he'd probably still be getting away with it."

"Maybe he just wanted to help women have babies," said Maddy. "You paint him as a devil but in his heart, he may have thought he was doing good."

Jessica said, "Deceiving his own patients? Spreading his seed like he did? That's pure ego, I'm sorry. I'm glad I never met him."

"Aren't you curious? Wouldn't you like to see him and see if his mannerisms are like yours or if his tastes and hobbies are like yours?"

"Frankly, no. We can connect with our half-siblings and have contact with them. That'd answer some questions about heredity. If you want, I'll see if at some point Jeff would be willing to drive up from New York and meet us."

"That would be interesting, but I'd still like to meet our father."

"Maddy, it's not a good idea. You don't want to visit him in prison, it's icky. I'd stay far away. He sounds like a major manipulator and you don't want to get caught in his claws."

Emily spotted Rona Smyth entering the dining room with the young man they'd seen her with at Smyth Haven. "Look! That's Rona Smyth. I'll bet she's here to spy on Coralee."

"Her date looks young enough to be her son," said Jessica.

"Girls, stop the gossiping. Here's our food." Henry took the plate from Summer. "Do you have sugar-free syrup?"

"Of course. A lot of people, myself included, are watching out for sugar."

When she'd left, Emily said, "Watching out for sugar? Do you think…"

"Not everyone who mentions avoiding sugar has diabetes, Em. A girl her age is likely more worried about not gaining weight, right Maddy?"

"Why are you asking me? Do I look like I need to watch my weight?"

"Sam, see what you've got to look forward to if you get married and have kids? Women!"

"That does it. I'm only having sons." He dug into his omelet. "Delicious omelet."

Emily glanced over at Rona. She and her jail bait were engaged in a lively chat from the looks of it. Sick how they kept leaning in toward each other.

Sam said, "Excuse me a minute. Where's the rest room?"

Henry said, "Over by the lobby."

"How are things going with Sam?" said Emily.

"I don't know. I think he's seeing other women. Not that we said we're exclusive or anything, it just makes me uncomfortable."

"How do you know he's seeing other women?" asked Maddy.

"He rushes off to errands or meetings after school sometimes. We'll have dinner plans and he says he got held up in a parent conference. I don't see parents flocking to have conferences with the once a week technology teacher. What would you think?"

Maddy said, "Sounds like he's cheating on you."

"Yet when a guy even looks my way he puts his arm around me and acts all possessive."

Maddy said, "I know what you're saying. Look over there. He's flirting with the waitress."

Emily looked. Summer Martin was smiling. So was Sam. What was that paper he just handed her? His phone number?"

Henry said, "There are plenty of fish in the sea. Perhaps you need a new pond. I mean, how many male teachers are at the school?"

"Two."

"My point exactly. I'll introduce you to some of the residents around the hospital if you'd like."

"Thanks, but we'll see how this relationship plays out first."

Sam returned to the table. Emily said, "Now, if you'll excuse me a minute."

Emily walked over to the table where Rona and her date were eating omelets.

"Rona Smyth, the soup we bought from you the other day was delicious."

"Thanks. Not every day one of my favorite authors walks through the door. This is Kyle."

Kyle extended his hand. "Pleased to meet you."

At least he had manners. "Rona, I'd like you to be the subject of my next true crime book. Wait, not sure that came out right. What I mean is, I hear the gossip about you causing the accident that killed your parents."

"I didn't kill my parents!"

"I'm not saying you did. Perhaps we can work together and clear your name—maybe even find the real cause of the accident."

"Well, that would be a great relief. We can talk. Drop by Smyth Haven tomorrow."

"Will do. Enjoy your breakfast. Nice meeting you, Kyle."

Emily returned to the table. "Trying to line up an interview with the subject of my next book." She watched Rona and Kyle get up and leave the dining room. She hoped they weren't planning on replicating Coralee's omelets.

Coralee stopped at their table. "Hope you're all enjoying brunch."

"Absolutely," said Sam. "Jessica and I will be back frequently."

Coralee tuned to Maddy. "We got a whole litter of kittens and the Mama cat last night. Stop by and see."

"I will."

Emily said, "Jessica and Sam should see the cat café."

"Our talented daughter not only won the Science ribbon, she came up with a successful community project last year. Quite impressive." Henry speared the last bit of pancake off his plate.

"I'm done eating and I'd love to see the kittens," said Jessica.

They settled the bill, then visited the cat café. The kittens played with crinkled foil balls, while Mama cat stretched out on the top of the sofa. The others played in the cat tree.

Jessica picked up an orange kitten and rubbed her face against his fur. "Oh my goodness, I'm in love." She looked at Sam. "In love with this kitty."

"That's Tito." Maddy pet Mama cat. Henry tossed the foil balls to the babies.

"Maddy, how do you stop yourself from bringing them all home?"

"Chester's used to be an only child. He doesn't do well with other pets."

"I can't believe you started this place. What a great idea."

Another guest entered the café with her son. He picked up Tito, the kitten Jessica had just set down.

"Sam, do you want to hold one?" Maddy held a gray tabby to his face.

Sam took a step back. "No, I'm not much of a cat person."

Jessica took the kitten from Maddy. "Such a sweetie. Are they old enough to be away from their mother?"

"Yes. They look to be around three months old. Why don't you adopt one?"

"Me? Well, truth is I'd love to have a little companion. I was thinking about getting a pet."

"Take two!"

Jessica went over to the mama cat and snuggled against her fur. "I'm going to do it. In fact, I'm going to take Mama cat and the little gray tabby. The tabby's been playing with the little black kitten. Must be his brother. It's too hard to decide."

Sam said, "Are you sure? Cats scratch the furniture and the litter boxes stink."

"I'm sure. In fact, I'm taking three."

Maddy said, "That's so great. I'll help you with anything you need. The adoption application is over there on the desk."

"Hold Stripes while I fill it out."

"Stripes?"

"She looks like a Stripes. And this one is Ebony. I don't know what to call the mama yet."

Jessica filled out the paperwork while Maddy ran to tell Coralee the good news. It would take a day or two for the Humane Society, their partner in the café, to go over the paperwork and approve it.

Emily said, "You should go with Jessica to pick up cat supplies."

"I will."

Maddy went with Jessica to get the cat supplies. Henry and Emily headed home.

"What do you think about Sam?" asked Emily.

"What do you mean? He seems okay."

"I don't trust him. I saw him hand a note to Summer Martin. I'll bet it was his phone number. When she came to take our order he didn't act like he'd ever met her before."

"Jessica has a good head on her shoulders. She'll figure it out."

"How do you go from investment banking into teaching? Why didn't he get another job in the financial industry?"

"I don't know how easy those jobs are to find."

"I can't see him enjoying children."

"Why? Because he doesn't like cats?" Henry parked the Jeep and they went inside. Emily took off her coat and grabbed her laptop. She googled Fielding Construction.

"What are you doing?"

"The night of the science fair, Sam dropped a business card." She took it from her purse and showed him.

"So? Maybe he wants to have a house built."

"Then why is he using a company based in Chicago? Look at the address."

"Maybe the father of one of his students gave it to him."

Emily searched. "Aha. Do you know what Fielding Construction specializes in?"

"Miniature houses? Hospitals? How do I know?"

"Charter schools. This article says the company has partnered with Horace Mann Charter and they're the leaders in opening schools throughout the country."

"So he may be looking for another job. What's the problem?"

"He was complaining about the state of public schools at breakfast. He was an investment banker. Faith Maguire blocked the building of a charter school here in Sugarbury Falls, but I read in the paper the other day that construction is underway. According to this article I'm reading, Horace Mann Charter is the fastest growing company in the US right now."

"Why was Faith trying to block it?"

"Because tax money then has to be shared. Public schools lose funding and they're strapped for money as it is. We live in a small school district. I can't see why we need another school. Maddy's classes aren't full. In fact, the school didn't offer calculus this year due to under enrollment."

"You think Sam was investing in the charter school?"

"Or the construction company. If he had invested in either the school or the company it would have lost a small fortune. With Faith Maguire out of the picture, look what happened. She's dead and right away construction is moving forward."

"You don't even know that he invested in it."

"I know who could help us figure it out."

"Are you going to bother Rebecca again?"

"She enjoys helping me. Where's that bottle of wine we never opened at dinner?" She rummaged through the fridge. "I'll bring this over. Are you coming?"

"No, thanks. I'm going to grab a beer and watch some basketball."

"Suit yourself."

She called Rebecca first. Rebecca was only too happy to help. She kissed Henry on the cheek. "Last chance to get in on some spy work."

"Have fun."

Emily walked over to Rebecca and Abby's. When the door opened, the aroma of fresh cinnamon rolls made her stomach growl, in spite of the plentiful brunch.

"Abby's rolls just came out of the oven. Want one?"

"I shouldn't. But I will. And I brought wine. You and Abby can have it with your dinner."

"So, what are we hunting for?" She opened her laptop and pictures of foster children filled the screen. "Abby and I are thinking of adopting through the foster care system."

"That's wonderful! You'd be great parents."

Abby said, "We've been talking about it for some time. We knew before we got married we wanted a family someday. My photography business is really picking up, and with our flexible hours, I think we can handle it."

"If you need a reference, let us know."

"Now, what are we searching for?"

"Fielding Construction, Horace Mann Charter Schools, and Sam Benson."

"Okay. Let's start with Fielding Construction. Give me a minute. Looks like they're making a fortune building charter schools all over the country."

"I know. Can you get a list of investors?"

"Give me a few more minutes. Hmm. There are a lot of investors."

"Is Sam Benson one of them?"

She scrolled through the list. "Sure is. He invested oodles."

"Before or after Faith's death?"

"Before. Months before. In fact, when did he start working here? You said this was his first year, right?"

"He said he moved here last summer to start the school year."

"He invested well before then."

"Can you check out his employment record? He says he was an investment banker before he started teaching."

"Do you know what company he worked for?"

"No."

"Then have another cinnamon roll. This will take a few minutes."

Abby said, "I'll bet Maddy's enjoying having her sister here."

"She sure is. She's with her now buying cat supplies. Maddy showed her the cat café and Jessica is adopting two kittens and their mother."

"How wonderful."

"I'm hoping having her sister here will satisfy her curiosity."

"What do you mean?"

"I found out she's been receiving mail from her biological father."

"The doctor who was arrested?"

"Yep."

Rebecca said, "Got it!"

"What did you find out?"

"Your Sam Benson was fired from his banking job after he rolled his clients' money into an iffy proposition. The project went bust and they all lost money. The company fired him for not checking things out before he made the investment."

"If he lost his job, where did he get the funds to invest in Fielding Construction?"

"That was a good paying job. Single guy with that salary must have had a hefty savings." She clicked keys on her laptop. "Yep, I'll say. I got his bank records here. But he invested almost all of it into this construction company/charter school duo."

"If it didn't succeed, he'd have been broke?"

"Looks that way. He stands to make a fortune off the charter school expansion."

"Motive. Faith would have put an end to that dream."

"Not saying an investment banker turned technology teacher has the stomach for murder, but the incentive certainly existed."

"Thanks, Rebecca."

"Anytime."

Emily zipped her coat and walked around the bend. When she got to her driveway, something didn't look right. She picked up the pace. The front door was open. She ran inside.

"Henry? Henry, where are you?" She looked around the living room. "Henry?" Butterflies churned inside her. She heard cheering. The basketball game was on TV. Henry never would leave the house with the front door open and TV on. She called up the loft.

"Henry?"

Two rungs at a time, she flew up to the master bedroom. Maybe he decided to take a nap. The bed was made as she left it. She checked the master bathroom. Empty. Chester flew out from under the bed and ran down the ladder.

She went back downstairs and into the kitchen. "Henry!" Henry was lying on the floor, blood seeping from a wound on the back of his head. She knelt down. "Henry!" Her voice reached a volume she hadn't known existed.

Thank God he was still breathing. She gently shook him, but he didn't wake up. She grabbed her phone, hands shaking, and called 911.

"Henry, wake up!" He began to stir. His eyes slowly opened. "Where am I?"

"Henry, it's me. You're home. In the kitchen." Her knees felt sticky and she noticed shards of amber glass on the floor. "Do you remember what happened?"

He tried to sit up, then clutched his head and curled back down into a fetal position. "Aww, this hurts like a..."

She grabbed a dishtowel and held it to his wound. "Stay still. The ambulance is on the way."

"Emily, Dad? Where are you?" Maddy ran into the kitchen, followed by Jessica and Sam.

She knelt beside Henry. "Dad! Are you okay? What happened?"

"I'll call 911," said Sam.

"They're already on the way."

Jessica said, "What happened? Did he slip and fall?"

"I don't know. I was at Rebecca and Abby's. When I pulled in, the front door was open and I called his name but he didn't answer. I found him like this."

Henry grunted. "Help me up."

"Dad, stay still. Help's on the way."

Emily was relieved to hear sirens approaching. The EMTs rushed through the door, followed by Detectives Megan and Ron. "He's in the kitchen."

"Emily, what happened?"

"Megan, I came home and found the TV on and the front door open. He was unconscious in front of the fridge, right where he is now. The floor is sticky. Looks like he went to the fridge for a beer and someone hit him over the head. Be careful of the glass. He's bleeding. I put pressure to stop the bleeding—Maddy's holding the towel against it."

"Is anything missing?" asked Detective Ron.

"I...I don't know." She noticed Henry's wallet on the coffee table and checked through it. "His credit cards are still here, and two twenty dollar bills. And his phone is here, too." She scanned the living room.

"Wait! My laptop! It was on the chair by the fireplace. It's gone."

"Are you sure that's where you left it?"

"Positive. It was cold when I woke up. I started a fire and sat there in the chair to work."

"Anything else?"

"I have jewelry upstairs."

"Can you check and see if it's missing?"

"First, let me see Henry." She ran into the kitchen. By now Henry was sitting up with an icepack on his head. "Is he okay?"

The paramedic said, "I'd like to get him checked out at the hospital, but he's refusing. He may have a concussion."

Henry said, "I'll be fine."

"Henry, you might need stitches. And what if there's internal damage?"

"Em, I'm a doctor. The bleeding has already stopped. There's nothing they can do at the hospital except monitor me and I can do that here. Besides, no way am I leaving you and Maddy alone in this house."

Ron said, "Emily, can you check and see if anything's missing from the bedroom? And Maddy, check your room."

Emily ran up the ladder. Her gold necklace was sprawled across the dresser where she'd left it and her diamond bracelet was on top of her jewelry box. Satisfied nothing had been taken, she went back downstairs.

"Nothing's missing."

Maddy came out of her room. "My laptop is on my bed where I left it."

Sam said, "The lock is broken. I'll replace it for you. You shouldn't be in an unsecured home ever and particularly not after this."

Megan came inside. "I checked the perimeter. I found motorcycle tracks leading from the road to your driveway. I'll get an impression made."

The paramedic led Henry to the sofa. "He's all yours. He won't let us take him to the hospital. Watch out for dizziness, worsening headache, nausea…I wouldn't be surprised if he has a concussion."

Megan said, "Do you remember anything? Did you get a look at the attacker?"

"No. It was halftime so I went into the kitchen for a beer and next thing I know I feel this excruciating pain and feel myself hit the floor. Must have blacked out until Emily found me."

Ron said, "Halftime? Means this happened less than an hour ago. Emily, you're lucky he wasn't here waiting when you got home. I'm going to have a look around outside."

"He took my laptop. If he was in and out that quickly, he had to have known that's what he wanted to take. Henry, how didn't you hear him break the lock?"

"The volume was up, and I was in the kitchen. He had to have been quick and quiet."

"The intruder came specifically for my laptop. Henry, could it have been a woman?"

"I suppose. Like I said, I never saw him—or her."

"I told Rona Smyth I wanted to interview her for my book. I'll bet she had a change of heart and stole my computer so I would lose my notes."

Megan said, "I'll go question her when we're done here."

Ron came back in. "I found a shoe print. Looks like an athletic shoe."

Emily said, "Could it be from a woman's shoe?"

"Looked rather large—more like a man's shoe."

Megan said, "We'll get right on this. Did you lose all your notes?"

"Everything is backed up on the Cloud, thank God. Worst comes to worst I'll have to buy another laptop."

"Sam is almost done fixing your front door lock. Are you going to be okay here?"

"Yes. The intruder got what he—or she—was after. There's no need to come back here."

"Then Ron and I will get moving. I'll call you with any updates. Keep the doors locked."

"Thanks."

Emily helped Henry into the recliner. "Can I get you anything? Aspirin?"

"That would be good. Don't look at me like that. I'm fine."

Maddy sat on the sofa. "Want me to find a movie?"

"Sure. Nothing violent."

When Emily saw them watching a movie, she made a batch of microwave popcorn and settled in next to them. When dinner time rolled around, Maddy suggested pizza. Emily didn't feel like cooking and quickly agreed.

"That's my phone." Emily picked up her vibrating phone. "Megan, any news? Really? You're sure? Okay then."

"What did she say?" said Henry.

"She went over to Smyth Haven. Rona hadn't left the inn at all. A dozen guests confirmed her alibi."

Chapter 22

Emily filled Chester's bowl. As she got up, Henry came in for breakfast. "Henry, how are you feeling?" She looked at his head, parting the hair around the wound. "You have quite a bump, but no more bleeding."

Henry swallowed a couple of Excedrin. "I'm good. Just a bit of lingering headache. Did Maddy get off to school?"

"Yes. You're not going to the hospital today, are you?"

"I told them to call if they're short-handed. Otherwise, no. Want me to start price shopping for laptops?"

"I'm hoping it will be found quickly, but truth is, I can't do any work without it. I suppose if I get a new one and the police recover mine, I can bring it into school. I hate the desktop in my office."

"Aren't you running late?"

"My TA is covering for me this morning. I need to get over to Smyth Haven and interview Rona." She looked at her phone. It was early, but she hoped to get her test results today. "I'm going to get over there. The breakfast rush will be about over."

When she got to Smyth Haven, Rona brought her into her office. A musty oak desk sat smack in the middle of the room.

"Is that an antique?"

"I don't think so. This was my father's office when he was alive. When we renovated, I had them leave this office just as it was when Dad was alive. Makes me feel connected to him."

Emily fished a legal pad from her oversized purse. "Tell me about the accident."

"Well, I had just moved home for a while. My restaurant, The Silver Spoon, had burned to the ground and I needed to figure out what to do next."

"You received insurance money, correct?"

"Not immediately, but yes. I was starting to look for another location when the accident happened."

"Were you at home when you heard the news?"

"Yes. I'd fallen asleep watching a movie when I heard knocking on the door. It was really late. I wasn't about to open it, but when they said it was the police, well, I had a bad feeling in the pit of my stomach."

"They came in and said your parents had an accident? Swerved into the lake? What words did they use?"

"They told me to sit down, that they had bad news. I barely remember the words. It was such a blur. All I know is they said my parents were dead."

"How awful. Where had they been that evening?"

"They'd gone to dinner, and to see a play. The police said Dad didn't even try to stop. There were no skid marks. I figure he must have had a stroke or something."

"Did they find that in the autopsy?"

"No, they didn't. He was a good driver. I thought he'd fallen asleep at the wheel since they found no medical cause."

"Why did they suspect foul play?"

"They said the car had been tampered with. I'd had a huge fight with them earlier that day, right in the middle of the street down town. Who else had a motive? Everyone loved them both."

"Did they have any evidence it was you?"

"All circumstantial. Tools. A few key tools were missing from the garage wall. Dad had them hung in specific, labeled spots. He was a little OCD."

"Tools that could have been used to tamper with the car."

"Yes."

"Did they locate those tools?"

"Nope."

"Do you think someone deliberately caused the accident?"

"I can't imagine it. They'd had brake problems in that car before. As a matter of fact, they'd just had them repaired shortly before the accident."

"And the missing tools?"

"I don't want this made public, but my father was suffering from dementia. I think he misplaced the tools, maybe even fiddled with the car himself thinking he was repairing it. It also explains him zoning out while driving."

"But your mother was in the car, too."

"One drink and she'd have been out like a light. At least that's what I tell myself. I don't think either of them realized what was happening. I hope they didn't."

"I heard that you were suspected of starting the fire at The Silver Spoon to collect the insurance money."

Rona's raised her voice. The veins in her neck showed. "I absolutely did not burn down my own restaurant. The police investigated. No foul play."

"But the original report from the fire department states there was evidence of an accelerant found at the scene."

"That's not true. Read the insurance report. Had that been true, why would the insurance company have paid out the claim? I thought you were on my side. That's why I agreed to this interview."

Emily considered challenging her—admitting to having seen the bank records. She opted against it. Why show all her cards at once? Besides, if Rona got angry at her, that'd been the end of her cooperation and the book would be that much harder to write. Rona might even try to stop it from being written altogether.

"I'm not saying I believed what I heard. Rumors fly in situations like that."

Rona lowered her voice. "Yes, they do. I loved my parents. Now, I have to get back to work."

"Thanks for your time. May I contact you if I have questions down the road?"

"If I'm not too busy."

"And if you think of anything else that may be relevant, here's my card. It'd be wonderful if we could clear your name once and for all—find out what really happened that night."

It was a start. Emily was surprised. She got a vibe that Rona did love her parents and that she was telling the truth. Then again, she obviously bribed the insurance investigator—based on the bank record evidence uncovered by Rebecca. And she was on the brink of bankruptcy.

Rona went back to the dining area. On her way out, Emily noticed a ski jacket hanging on the coat rack by the galoshes. She zeroed in on the zipper. The bottom piece, the part you pulled to zip and unzip, was missing! It had to be Rona's jacket. The guests kept theirs in their rooms surely. Rona had spied on Coralee after all. She hustled out to the car.

Her phone buzzed. When she looked at the caller ID, her heart stopped. It was the breast center. She took a moment to calm herself, then answered.

"Is this Mrs. Emily Fox?"

"It is." The words stuck in her throat.

"I have your test results."

"Go on."

"Good news. There's no evidence of a tumor at this time. We'd like you to follow up in six months with another ultrasound and compression just to be certain."

"So I don't have cancer?"

"No. Keep up with your screenings, though."

"I will. Thank you, Doctor."

She let out a scream, right there in the car. She was okay. No cancer. Then again, she'd have to follow up in six months, not the usual year between screenings. Why? Never mind. It was good news. She shouldn't have worked herself into a tizzy the way she had. As a matter of fact, the news was so good, she decided to take herself out to lunch.

She drove downtown and pulled in front of the Wildflower Bistro, which connected to a used book store. She sat in a booth and studied the lunch menu. A mushroom and sprouts sandwich on wheat bread...or a cranberry and goat cheese salad? She opted for the sandwich. She rarely ate lunch downtown and was looking forward to her own private celebration. Maybe even a glass of wine.

Through the front window, she saw Sam walking with Summer Martin. Was he cheating on Jessica already? They were stopping at the door of the bistro. They were coming inside! She slumped down and hid behind the menu.

The waitress seated them in the booth right behind hers. She didn't want to be seen—sure Sam wouldn't be comfortable knowing she'd run back and tell Jessica. Of course that was exactly what she had in mind.

Without too much straining, she overheard their conversation.

"Everything's moving ahead. Won't be long before we're both rich."

"What if they find out, you know?"

"They won't."

"If that witch Faith Maguire was still alive, our whole plan would be up in smoke."

"But she's not. She got what was coming to her."

"I visited my parents at the prison. I actually saw Mom smile when I told her the news."

"We're all better off now that Faith Maguire is dead. What are you ordering for lunch?"

"The quiche and salad looks good. Tired of eating the same old same old at the inn. Coralee prides herself in her cooking, but if that food wasn't free for us employees…Let's say I don't see how she stays in business."

Jessica was right to be wary of this guy. When she finished her lunch, she slipped out while Sam and Summer were still plotting. What was Sam's alibi the night Faith was murdered? She headed to the police station. Megan waved her into her office.

"Megan, I overheard Sam Benson and Summer Martin talking. They both have money invested in the new charter school and I think they plotted to kill Faith Maguire. She was the single roadblock to the school moving forward. Summer was right at the inn that night. Can you check and see if Sam has an alibi?"

"Emily, calm down. We interviewed Summer Martin and she was in her room the whole evening—after Coralee took her off waitress duty. We interviewed everyone who was there that night and no one saw her go back into the kitchen."

"She could have slipped out her window. Why would anyone remember her leaving the room?"

"The employee rooms aren't on the ground floor. We didn't see her on CCTV leaving or entering the inn."

"What about Sam Benson?"

"His name never came up. What makes you think he was at the inn that night?"

"It's just...the smugness when he talked to Jessica—like he had something to do with, as he called it, 'removing the roadblock'."

"We can't randomly question someone who was nowhere near the murder scene. I'm sorry."

"Can you look into his financial records? He's invested a lot of money in the charter school/construction company partnership."

"How do you know that?"

"I...um...he said so." She wasn't about to admit to having a clandestine spy as a neighbor.

"Sorry, Emily. I can't do that on a whim."

"So what do you have so far? Dave Maguire had motive, but he was at an AA meeting at the time. Did you check out his alibi? He lied about when he arrived in town. Dave seemed sincere when he admitted to his drinking issues and Emily had believed him, but just to be thorough..."

"Yes. The husband, or ex-husband is always on the suspect list. He lied because he wasn't supposed to be near the girls."

"He's a father. I guess you can't blame him for wanting to see his daughters."

"He violated the custody agreement but he didn't kill anyone. Half a dozen witnesses placed him at the AA meeting during the time of the murder."

"And Arturo Rivera turned out to be a saint feeding the homeless people."

"Rona Smyth? Adding drops of Visine to her opponent's fondant at a baking competition? Oh, and she smokes. Ashes were found on the window ledge outside Coralee's dining room window. And she's missing the metal clasp off her jacket zipper."

"Emily, we appreciate your insights, and your hunches are often spot on, however, you have to trust us to do our jobs."

"And what about the red mud on her galoshes? And her boyfriend? Did you check out the motorcycle we saw leaving the Smyth Haven parking lot?"

"Emily, you're overstepping your bounds. You sound like you don't trust us at all to do our jobs."

"I do. I just feel for those poor girls left without their mother."

"Rest assured, we're going to find the killer." Her desk phone lit up. "I've got to take this call."

"Okay, thanks for your time."

Emily knew exactly where to head next. She stopped at Rebecca and Abby's.

"Rebecca, I overheard Jessica and Sam talking. They sound like they are in collusion over the murder."

"The murder? Or the investment scheme?"

"Both. Well, I don't know yet. That's why I came to you."

"Okay. I have a few minutes, but then I have a project I need to finish or I'll lose my day job."

"Can you look at Summer Martin's financials? How much did she invest in the charter school project and where did she get the money? She's a college student."

"I suppose she has control over whatever money her parents had before being arrested. Let's see..." As usual, it took only a few clicks before Rebecca had information. Emily had great admiration for Rebecca's skills.

"She has a good-sized bank account. Her parents' accounts list her as a joint owner. Wow. She put a lot of cash into this project. Made two huge withdrawals which were sent to Fielding Construction."

"And the company is profitable, right?"

"Oh, yeah. They're cleaning up around the country. This Vermont school, however, is the first expansion into the Northeast."

"Sam Benson says he quit investment banking to become a teacher. Is that true? I mean, that's quite a cut in salary, right?"

"Where did you say he lived before coming here?"

"Florida. Miami, I think."

"Do you know the name of the company he worked for?"

"No, sorry."

After a few minutes, Rebecca had the information she needed. "Sam Benson worked for Planet Wide Investments. He was fired, he didn't quit."

"Fired? Why?"

"He invested his clients' money into a risky investment without doing his homework. The investment went belly-up and the clients lost tons of money. Planet Wide had no choice but to get rid of him."

"How long ago was that?"

"Just last year."

"So he knows he won't be able to get another banking job and so he becomes a teacher."

"He did a quick certification program back in Florida. They're desperate for teachers down there— apparently the pay is one of the lowest in the country."

"But if he was certified in Florida, how could he teach here in Vermont? Certification is state by state."

"Vermont allows for a temporary certificate while specific requirements are met."

"He was lucky to find a job here. Turnover is almost non-existent according to Jessica, Maddy's sister. She was lucky enough to walk into a position, too."

"I have a good friend who teaches at the middle school. She said Faith Maguire came with a reputation for cleaning house. She got rid of some veteran teachers before she even took her official position as superintendent."

"So Sam starts working here and invests in this charter school project. He gets Summer Martin to come aboard, probably others, too."

"Not anyone who did their research. Your normal investor types wouldn't touch it if Benson's name was involved."

"How about an alibi? The police say there's no reason to investigate Sam Benson and Summer Martin has witnesses saying she was in her room that night. Plus, she doesn't show up on CCTV footage."

"I can't help you there. Does he live alone?"

"As far as I know."

"You said Jessica dates him, right? Maybe you can start with her."

Emily couldn't help feeling disappointed. She wanted to wrap up this case. What about the motorcycle she and Henry saw at Smyth Haven? It had to be the one that tried to run her over and crash into their car. She had to go back to Smyth Haven.

If Rona saw her, it'd look suspicious. She carefully made her way to the inn, listening and watching. It was cold and the guests weren't gathered on the porch as they might have been on a milder day. The motorcycle wasn't in the parking lot so she inched her way around the back of the inn, careful to avoid the CCTV cameras. She noticed a garden shed at the back of the property and looking to make sure she wasn't being watched, she ran to it.

A rusty chain lock secured the door, however, the lock hung open. Around Sugarbury Falls, most people left their garages, sheds…even homes unlocked. She carefully freed the chain and pulled the shed ajar with a loud creak.

The damp, musty air made her cough. The rusty door had been difficult to open but she wished she'd pulled it a bit more so she could better see what was in here. A small stream of sunlight was all she had. Why had she left her phone in the car? The flashlight app would have helped.

The usual rakes and shovels leaned against one wall. Toward the back, burlap sacks and canvas sheets protected items from rust. Squinting, she walked toward a covered object that looked from its silhouette, exactly like a motorcycle! Her heart raced. If she could get the license number, maybe…

Emily screamed when the shed door creaked shut. The sliver of outside light was now gone. She heard the chain slam against the outside of the shed.

Chapter 23

"Who's there? Hello?" She groped her way to the door and pounded. "Help! Let me out of here!" Had Rona seen her come in here? Had she followed her?

"Help, somebody. Let me out!" She pounded on the door, then kicked at it, slammed against it with all her body weight. No one was coming. No one knew she was here. No one knew the shed existed, in all likelihood.

She groped her way back to the covered object and peeked underneath. A small stream of sunlight filtered through the space between the roof and the wall and her eyes adjusted to where she could kind of see. She ripped off the cover. A motorcycle—just as she thought. It had to be the one that chased her. Why else would someone hide it in here rather than leave it in the parking lot? She bent down and squinted at the license plate, trying to memorize the number. The wheels were caked in dirt, just as the galoshes had been.

How was she going to get out? She banged the walls. Thin metal. She needed something capable of cutting through them—hedge clippers? A machete? She stood on the frozen dirt which served as the shed floor. The shovel! She grabbed it, stepped on it, pushed with her foot. Using all the might and determination she could muster, she couldn't penetrate the cold ground. She tried a second time with the same result.

She looked around the shed and spotted a crate. She pulled it over and stood on it to get more leverage, then pushed against the top of the shovel. She felt the shovel crack through the ground. Excited, she did it again. And again.

After three attempts, she'd hardly made a dent in it. It was like trying to scoop sand off a beach with a cup. Discouraged, she sat on the crate to think.

The toolbox! She opened the lid. A hammer! She banged it against the metal door trying to break through the metal but found it impossible. She rummaged through the toolbox for a screwdriver and tried to pry open the locked door. Fruitless. She felt like crying.

The chain clanged against the shed. Had someone heard her hammering the metal walls? She jumped to her feet.

The door creaked open as it slid in the rusty track. "Going somewhere?"

Emily squinted. Then she realized who it was. Kyle. Rona's boyfriend.

"You have to let me out of here. I have friends on the police force and they know I'm here. Do you want to be arrested for kidnapping?"

"You're not going anywhere." In the sliver of light, she saw a glint of metal. He was holding a shotgun. She felt as if her heart would burst through her chest.

"All I wanted was to see if the motorcycle was in here. Was it you who tried to kill me? Did you throw the rock through my window and try to run my husband and me off the road?"

"I warned you. You should have listened. Not too smart for a college professor, or worse—a reporter."

"If you let me go, I won't press charges. In fact, I'm writing the book which could prove your girlfriend is innocent."

"My girlfriend?"

The door creaked open further and a flood of sunlight illuminated the interior of the shed. Emily rubbed her eyes. "Rona? Please tell your boyfriend to let me go." She prayed they weren't in this together.

"My boyfriend? Kyle what are you doing in here?"

"I'll take care of her, Mom. Don't worry."

"Mom? She's your mother?" Emily tried to digest the words.

"Yeah, and I won't let her go to jail."

Rona said, "What are you talking about, Kyle? Why would I go to jail?"

"I'll always have your back, Mom. I won't let this reporter ruin your reputation. I did it for you. That's why I rigged up the car that night."

"What car? What are you talking about?"

"The car Grandpa was driving. You know—the night of the accident."

Rona's hands flew to her mouth. "You? No. Tell me you didn't."

"I love you, Mom. I'd do anything for you."

Rona shook her head. "Tell me you didn't kill your own grandparents. How..."

"I had to. I heard you arguing with Grandpa. He refused to turn the house into a bed and breakfast. You told him we'd be out on the street if he didn't but he still said no."

"But I would have..."

"And the insurance money didn't cover the cost of buying a new restaurant."

"But they were my parents! My flesh and blood!"

"Then you know how I feel about you. I knew you'd be successful if you could just start over. I was right."

"Kyle, put down the gun."

"Did you set fire to the Silver Spoon, too?" asked Emily.

"I thought the insurance money would be more. Mom knew about it."

"Only after the fact." She turned to Emily. "I used the bulk of that money to bribe the insurance adjuster so Kyle wouldn't go back to jail."

"Back to jail?"

"He's had his share of trouble. Growing up without a father in the picture is tough."

"Tough enough to justify murder? He killed his own grandparents. Rona, you have to turn him in. To top it off, he killed Faith Maguire."

Kyle said, "Who?"

"The woman who died from eating the tainted cheesecake. You wanted to make sure your mother's business would be a success so you tried to get rid of the competition. After all, who'd chose to eat at the Outside Inn after a woman ate there and died?"

"Kyle, is that true?" Rona sounded shocked.

Emily said, "We found ashes on the ledge, and a piece of a broken zipper. Rona, I know you were there, looking in the dining room window. You knew about this."

Rona said, "Whoa! I did do a bit of spying to see why the Outside Inn was so successful. Yes, I peeked in the window, but murder? How dare you accuse me."

"Mom's not a killer," said Kyle.

"But you are. If you don't go to the police it'll be worse. You killed three people already and if you kill me, too..." Her legs felt like Jell-O, but she managed to keep her voice steady.

Kyle took a step closer, still aiming the shotgun at Emily's head. "I admit to killing my grandparents but this Faith woman? I don't know what you're talking about. You ain't gonna pin that on me."

"Someone snuck into Coralee's place and injected her cheesecake with a diabetes medication. A common one. Your mother said she had issues with sugar. Was she on medication by any chance?"

182 The Tainted Course

Rona said, "I never said I'm diabetic. Overweight, maybe, but diabetic?"

"Then Kyle, you had access to all the guests at Smyth Haven. It wouldn't have been too difficult to find enough medication to do the deed."

"What deed? You'd better shut up. Yes, I killed my grandparents, but I had nothing to do with poisoning cheesecake. That's just crazy." He took a step closer. "Mom, go back to the inn. You don't need to see this."

Rona pleaded, "Kyle, you need help. I'll hire a lawyer. We'll show the court you're ill and get you the help you need."

"Mom, go away. I don't want you to see this. Go. Now!" He stepped closer to Emily and cocked the gun.

Emily's heart raced. She watched Rona turn toward the shed door. Hope exhausted, Emily said a quick prayer and begged for her life. "I'm a mother. I have a daughter."

Kyle took another step closer. She held her breath, terrified that this would be her last moment. Then... Rona turned around wielding the shovel and whacked Kyle over the head. He slumped into a heap on the dirt floor. Emily shook. She was paralyzed for a moment, then ran to Rona. "You saved my life."

"And my life is over. My parents are dead, my own son killed them...he'll be in jail for the rest of his life." She took out her phone and called the police.

Chapter 24

"Emily, are you all right?" said Megan. "What happened here?"

"Kyle had me hostage and was about to kill me. Rona saved my life. Kyle is Rona's son. He's responsible for killing his grandparents."

"Do you need medical attention?"

"No, I'm fine."

"Come down to the station. We'll need a statement. Rona, you have to come with us also."

"But my son...he's mentally ill. Don't throw him in jail, he needs help."

"We'll iron everything out later. I know for sure he kidnapped Emily and was holding her against her will."

"He held a shotgun to my head, Megan. If Rona hadn't incapacitated him and called the police, you'd be looking at another murder."

Kyle was arrested, and Emily rode to the station with Megan. Henry and Maddy were waiting outside when the patrol car pulled in front of the station.

"Emily, we were worried sick, Maddy and I. Are you okay?"

"I'm fine. I just want to get this over with and go home."

"You told Henry you'd be more careful. I heard you say it. Don't I matter enough for you to make sure you stay alive?"

"Maddy, I'm so sorry. I didn't mean to..."

"Maddy, we have to get your mother's statement. It shouldn't take long," said Megan.

Back at home, Henry immediately started a fire. Emily sat on her sofa wrapped in an afghan.

"You could have been killed. When you didn't answer your phone and didn't come home, I knew something was wrong. I thought you promised not to take chances like that? You heard how upset you made Maddy."

Mad at herself, especially after finding out she'd escaped a cancer diagnosis, she said, "I'm so sorry."

Maddy came in with a cup of tea. "Are you warm enough? I can get another blanket from the closet."

"I'm fine." She took the tea and set it on the coffee table. "Come here." She hugged Maddy, tightly. She never wanted to let go. "I'm sorry, baby. I shouldn't have taken a chance like that. I'll be here for you, always."

"It's okay. I know you were trying to help Ava and find out who killed her mother."

Now that her mind had a chance to clear, it dawned on Emily. If Kyle didn't kill Faith, the killer was still at large! *If* Kyle was telling the truth.

"Henry, Kyle freely admitted to killing his grandparents and setting fire to the Silver Spoon, but he swore he didn't kill Faith."

"The guy's sick in the head. I wouldn't believe him."

"He had no problem admitting to the other murders."

"I'm sure Megan and Ron will get to the bottom of it. Just relax." He pushed the hassock over and lifted her feet onto it."

Maddy said, "Ava's moving back to Georgia next week. She's pretty upset about it."

"I thought they were staying here, at least until the end of the school year?"

"Her Dad's boss called and said if he doesn't go back now, he's fired."

"Certainly he has to think about providing for the girls," said Henry.

"Is Tilly moving back with them? That will make the transition easier." Emily took a sip of her tea.

"She really wants to, but Ava's father said he didn't have the money to keep her on. Besides, he has family in Georgia to help with the girls. Ava said Tilly hasn't stopped crying since he made the announcement."

Emily said, "She really cares for those girls. She'll find another family who needs her and I'm sure she'll stay in touch with them."

Henry's phone vibrated. "Hi, Pat. Yes, she's fine. It could have ended much worse to be sure. I'll tell her. What? Chickened out again? You've got to take the bull by the horns and ask her to marry you before she gets fed up and finds someone new. Only kidding. Yes, I'll ask them. Take care, buddy."

"What did he chicken out of?" asked Emily. "Another aborted proposal attempt?"

"Yep. Poor guy's trying too hard. He should just simply ask her already."

Maddy said, "I think I have an idea."

"Well, don't kept it to yourself," said Henry.

"Megan's been taking a Spanish class all year."

Emily said, "I know. Her dream is to visit her relatives in Barcelona one day. She said so over dinner the other night."

"Give me a day to work on it." She got up, kissed Emily and Henry on the cheeks and said, "I'm going to bed now." She scooped up Chester.

Too exhausted to press further, Emily said, "Me, too."

Emily slept like a baby. In the morning, she woke to the aroma of coffee and decided to skip her run. Henry was working on his Sudoku when she went downstairs.

"You were out like a light last night," said Henry.

"Yesterday was quite a day."

"You can relax now."

"Not really. After all that, we still don't know who killed Faith."

"Megan and Ron will have to change direction but they'll solve this. With Kyle in jail, is your plan for your next book a no-go?"

"I think it would hurt Rona and doubt she'd consent to it. I'll find a new idea."

"I know you will."

Emily said, "With Rona off the suspect list, I wonder who they'll go after next."

"Sam Benson?"

"He's the only one of the original suspects without an alibi. And Summer. What if he and Summer worked together? She had access to the kitchen and they both stand to profit from the charter school project forging ahead."

Henry poured a second cup of coffee. "Not to change the subject, but Maddy wants us to keep tonight free. She has a surprise planned."

"A surprise?"

"She needs our help is all she said. She said something about dinner at the inn."

"Well, I'll take any excuse not to have to cook tonight. I do need to get to work, though. I've pawned off my class to my TA a little too often this semester." She looked out the window. "The weather is supposed to get bad. I was kind of hoping they'd cancel classes."

"I've got to get going, too." He finished his coffee and put the mug in the sink. "I'll see you tonight."

When Henry got to the hospital, a nurse told him that Tilly and Mila were waiting in a cubicle. He went to see them first.

"Tilly, what happened? Another seizure?"

"She says she threw up this morning in the bathroom. Her father is busy making arrangements to move them back to Georgia so I offered to bring her over."

Henry said, "Mila, did you actually throw up this time or just feel like you were going to, like last time?"

Mila crossed her arms over her chest and didn't answer.

"Mila, the doctor is talking to you. He can't help you if you don't talk to him."

Mila grunted and turned away. Henry tried to coax her to answer, but she refused.

"Mila, the doctor has lots of sick people who need his help. If you don't want him to help you, let's go. I can drop you off at school on my way home."

Mila said, "I don't want to move to Georgia. I want to stay here with you and be in Miss Pratt's class."

Tilly said, "Sweetheart, I'd love nothing more than for you to do just that, but your father has a job waiting. I'll visit you and we can do *Facetime* every single day." She turned to Henry. "I love this girl and her sister like they're my own."

"Do you have children of your own?"

Tilly looked away, appearing to compose herself before answering. "I did. I had a daughter. She's no longer with us. I'll never get over it."

"I'm so sorry. I didn't mean to…"

"Of course, you didn't. It's always hard when people ask me that. If I say no, I feel like I'm denying she ever existed. If I say yes, I have to explain."

Mila said, "I need the bathroom." She hopped out of bed.

"I'll take you."

Henry said, "No need. There's one right outside the cubicle." He pulled the curtain open. "Right there."

"I'm sorry we wasted your time."

"Not a problem. The little girl has been through a lot."

"And she's about to go through more. I told Dave to leave the girls here with me for the rest of the school year, but he refused."

"He probably needs them as much as they need him right now. He and Faith were on the outs but they were once married and in love. They had kids together. I'm sure he's grieving, too."

Mila came back into the cubicle. "Feeling better?" asked Tilly.

"Yeah. I want to go back to school."

"That's okay, right, Doctor Fox?"

"Sure. Bye, Mila. I think there are lollipops at the desk if it's okay with Tilly."

"Of course, it is," said Tilly. "Am I too old for one? Just kidding. My own doctor would kill me. I haven't been very good about monitoring my blood sugar."

"Are you diabetic?"

"Who isn't these days? I started on pills recently but my plan is to lose fifteen pounds and start walking once the weather warms up. Doctor says I should be able to control it that way and won't need the pills."

"Sounds like a plan."

"Let's go, Mila. Thanks again, Dr. Fox."

Henry finished with his patients, then went down to the morgue to visit Pat.

"Hey, buddy. How's Emily?"

"No worse for the wear. I could have killed her myself for getting herself in the situation she did. If Rona hadn't shown up…"

"But she did. And a killer is off the streets thanks to her."

"Too bad it isn't the killer she was after, but hey. She made Megan's job a little easier, right?"

"Speaking of Megan, your daughter left me a cryptic text."

"Maddy texted you?"

"She said Megan and I should meet you guys at the inn for dinner at 7 sharp and to dress nicely."

"Hmm. She did tell Em and me to keep tonight free."

"Spill it. What has she got in mind?" said Pat.

"I swear, I haven't a clue. Guess we'll find out together."

Pat's phone buzzed. "Hey, Megan. Yeah? Okay. You can still meet for dinner, right? Maddy says to dress up. She probably won an award or something. Yeah. Love you, too."

After he ended the call with Megan, Henry asked, "What award?"

"I don't know. She's always winning stuff, right? Anyhow, Megan says Kyle Smyth confessed to murdering his grandparents. He swore he had nothing to do with Faith Maguire's death. Megan says his alibi checks out for that night, just like his mother's. They were both eating dinner with a family friend."

"So what now?"

"They keep investigating. It's only been a couple of weeks. These things take time. Can you hand me my coffee?" He took a sip of the coffee and spit it out. "Yuck, too bitter. I thought I added sugar at home but I guess I didn't."

Henry froze, coffee in hand. "You normally add the sugar at home. This time, you have to add it here—not in your kitchen. You didn't add it in the kitchen. You're a genius!"

"That's been established. What in this moment impressed you? The fact I forgot to do what I do as a habit?"

"You forgot to add sugar in your kitchen, but you were able to add it here. What if Faith's killer didn't sneak into the kitchen to add the meds? Faith took her dessert home with her. What if someone added it back at her house, not at Coralee's?"

"I suppose you're right. It could have happened that way."

"That's a game changer. Instead of asking who had access to Coralee's kitchen, we should be asking who had access to Faith's kitchen! I've got to tell Emily."

"And is there anything you want me to tell Megan, since she is a detective and all?"

"Tell her to look at who had access to the medication as well as Faith's fridge."

Henry's half-day shift was nearly over. He checked to make sure the ER was under control, then got into his car. Did Dave Maguire poison the cheesecake? If the girls knew he was already in town, Ava may have left a door unlocked or given him a key. Faith had diabetes meds in the house. Tilly just admitted to having diabetes herself. Plenty of pharmaceuticals lying around to drop blood sugar. How many pills would he have needed to piece together a dose capable of killing Faith? He picked up the phone to call Emily, but realized she was still in class.

As soon as he got home, he took off his coat and found his drug reference handbook. Then he cross referenced the information with what he found on the pharmaceutical website. Whether or not Dave had enough pills to kill Faith depended on what Faith had left in her prescription bottle. He called Megan.

"Megan, I have a question for you. When the police gathered evidence from the Maguire house, how many pills were left in Faith Maguire's diabetes prescription? Sure, I'll wait."

He tried to determine how many pills Dave could have swiped without Tilly noticing. If Faith's prescription was nearly empty and was ready for a refill, he couldn't have come up with enough pills. However, if she'd recently had it filled, then..."

"Yes, Megan. I'm still here. The bottle was empty? Okay, look at the date of the last refill. She had just gotten a refill the day before she died? I think you need to consider bringing in Dave Maguire for questioning before he leaves town. Thanks, see you tonight."

Henry made himself a sandwich and continued the Sudoku he'd started before work. Emily and Maddy wouldn't be home for a couple of hours. Perhaps he'd even sneak in a nap.

Before he finished lunch, his phone buzzed.

"Maddy? Is everything okay? Maybe Ava didn't feel well and went home."

Maddy said, "We ate lunch together. She was fine and said she'd see me in geometry but she never showed."

"Is she skipping class? Maybe she didn't finish her homework and was afraid to get a zero or something."

"She'd never skip class. She'd have asked to copy mine instead. Besides, I texted Jessica. She said Mila is absent today."

"That's because she was at the hospital this morning. She had another anxiety attack—told Tilly she was going to throw up. She was worried about having to move back to Georgia. The three of us had a talk and Tilly was going to drop her off at school. She seemed fine when she left, but maybe Tilly changed her mind and took her home instead."

"Can you go over to their house and check? I tried calling Ava but it goes straight to voicemail and I don't have a number for the housekeeper."

"Okay. I'll take care of it and get back to you."

Henry went to his laptop and accessed the patient files to get a number for Tilly. When he called, it went to voicemail as well. He took Dave Maguire's number from the emergency contacts. Again, voicemail.

The last thing he felt like doing was trading his nap for a visit to the Maguire house, but Maddy was worried and he'd promised he'd look into it. Making it worse, freezing rain pelted his Jeep and he had to scrape ice off the windshield before taking off.

When he got to Ava's, the driveway was empty. He pulled up his hood and knocked on the front door. No answer.

He peeked in the window and saw a purse on the floor, contents spilling out. He recognized it as the purse Tilly was carrying at the hospital that morning. Why would she have left the house without it? And if she were to leave it behind, would she have left the contents all over the floor? Something wasn't right. She didn't leave voluntarily. Dave Maguire! What if he'd kidnapped them? What if he talked to Tilly and found out he'd questioned her about the diabetes meds?

He called Megan on the way home. He hoped the police could catch up with Dave Maguire before he skipped town. Where was Tilly's car? Dave must be driving it. He called Megan back to give her that piece of information.

When he got home, Emily was waiting.

"I thought you had office hours after class today."

"I did, but Maddy called and said she was worried Ava disappeared. She thought Ava might show up at our house."

"I was just over at the Maguire's. Tilly's car is gone and her purse is spilled out on the floor in the foyer."

"I tried calling Dave but it went to voicemail."

"I know. I think he kidnapped Tilly and the girls."

"Why? He has custody now."

"I saw Tilly and Mila in the ER again this morning. I asked Tilly about her diabetes meds and if it was the same thing Faith had taken. I don't know, but I think she may have spoken to Dave and he got suspicious."

"Of what?"

"Faith had just picked up a refill of her meds the day before she died. With what was in the bottle plus a few pills from Tilly, Dave could have snuck into the house and poisoned the cheesecake while it was in the fridge. I think he knows I figured it out."

"He stole pills from Tilly and Faith?"

"Yes. He's a bright guy. Surely he knew the risk of an overdose. Tilly takes a newer drug but it has the same effect—dropping blood sugar. And if it dropped during the night while Faith was asleep..."

"Okay. You called the police. Where is Dave taking them? Leaving the country?"

"He'd need passports and Mila is seven. I kind of doubt the kids have passports. And last minute plane tickets to anywhere would be expensive. Besides, Tilly isn't willingly getting on a plane. She'd alert the authorities as soon as she got inside the airport."

"So assume he's driving. He isn't familiar with the area. Where would he go?"

"If he's worried about being chased, he'll avoid the major highways. Canada?"

"Passports, remember?"

"I have no clue. I hope the police have an idea."

They both jumped when they heard someone pounding on the front door.

"I'll get it," said Henry. Emily followed him to the door. When he opened it, they both gasped. It was Dave Maguire!

Chapter 25

"Dave? Are the girls in the car? Is everyone all right?" asked Henry.

"Huh? Can I come in? I'm getting wet."

"The police are looking all over for you. If you turn yourself in now…"

"What are you talking about?" shouted Dave. "My girls are missing. The school called. Is Ava here?"

"No, we thought you had her," said Emily.

"Me? Why? They're supposed to be at school."

"We tried calling you but it went straight to voicemail."

"I was on the phone with my boss all morning. Had to be near a fax machine. Not easy to find a place with one around here. Had to work through some client issues. I'm lucky my boss gave me a few days to get back there."

"Did you talk to Tilly?"

"I called. She didn't pick up. Neither did Ava. I stopped here on my way home in case she was with Maddy. What's going on here?"

"Maddy called. Ava disappeared from school and Mila never showed up. I saw Mila at the hospital this morning."

"The hospital? What happened?"

"Another anxiety attack, like when you brought her in the other day. She's fine. Tilly was going to drop her off at school but she didn't. They aren't home and it looks like Tilly left in a hurry. Do you know where she may have taken the girls?"

"No! I told her as soon as the girls got home from school we needed to pack. I bought plane tickets for tomorrow."

"Was Tilly okay with you taking the girls back to Georgia?"

"What does that matter? She's just the housekeeper. She seemed sad. Practically begged me to take her with us, but I can't afford to do that. Besides, I have family to help in Georgia."

"Would she have run away with the girls? Is that possible?"

"I don't know her all that well. She seems very attached to them."

Emily said, "I'll call Megan and tell her Dave is with us. Meanwhile, let's go to the house. If Tilly kidnapped the girls, perhaps she left a clue as to where she was headed."

When they got to the house, Emily picked up the items on the foyer floor that had spilled out of the purse. "She sure left in a hurry. The wallet's gone, but she left the rest of her things here."

Dave flew up the stairs. "The girls' things are all here. The drawers are full and Ava's laptop is sitting on her bed. If they'd planned to leave, Ava would have taken it with her. Her phone charger is here too. She certainly would have packed it if she knew they were leaving."

What did Megan say?" asked Henry.

"They have an APB out for Tilly's car. They'll check credit card records. Eventually Tilly will need gas and food."

Dave said, "I found something. On the pad by Tilly's bed. She'd written something."

Emily said, "This is as old school as it gets, but give me a pencil."

Dave ran into Ava's room and found one the desk. "Here you go."

Emily scratched the lead back and forth across the pad until she could read what had been on it. "Bungalow Village, St. Johnsbury. That's not too far from here. Let's go."

"I'll call the police." said Emily.

"Fine, but we're going there, too."

Henry started the Jeep and Emily entered the address into the GPS.

"Hurry," said Dave. "What if she hurts the girls?"

"If she loves them as she seems to, she won't hurt them."

"Then why is she running?"

Henry said, "Because I think she killed Faith and she thinks the police are onto her."

"Killed Faith? Why on Earth?"

"Who knows. The important thing is finding her and the girls."

"Hurry up!" said Dave.

Henry stepped on the gas. It was sleeting heavily and he could feel the tires slipping as he accelerated. With laser focus, he drove as fast as he could, slowing down only when the car started skidding. *Slippery roads— Tilly is on the run. What if she crashes?* He kept his thoughts to himself.

Emily said, "Turn left at the next street. Henry, can you see out the windshield?"

The wipers, even on full speed, weren't meant to deflect pellets of ice. "I'm good."

"Turn right at the barn." Emily, sitting in back, could barely see out the window, but she heard sirens. "There's a crash up ahead. What if..."

Henry strained to see what had happened. He heard sirens. "It's not them. It's a truck. We're almost there, aren't we?"

"According to the GPS just a few more minutes," said Emily.

Henry watched the accident scene through the rearview mirror. "Looks like they're closing the road back there."

"What if the police can't get through?" said Dave. "Wat if we're all too late?"

"Turn here!"

Henry felt the tires slide. "You have to warn me, especially with these roads." He managed to steer into the skid and get the Jeep back on track.

Dave said, "That's it, right? Bungalow Village?"

"Yep." Henry pulled into the icy parking lot and all three ran to the office door.

"Can I help you?" asked an acne-suffering teen.

Dave said, "I'm looking for my girls. They're with a middle-aged woman. What room are they in? Give us the keys."

"I can't give them to you. Privacy and all..."

Dave grabbed him by the neck. "Tell me what cabin they're in." The veins popped from his neck.

Meanwhile, Emily snuck around the other side of the counter. "Cabin 123. Let's go."

The wind whipped ice pellets in Emily's eyes making it difficult to find the numbers. "Here it is. The light's on inside." She pounded on the door. A moment later, Henry and Dave were at her side. "Open up, Tilly. You don't want to hurt the girls." She heard sounds on the other side of the door, but no response.

Dave pounded. "Open up! Give me my girls, Tilly. This isn't right." He pounded and yelled but got no response.

Henry walked around the cabin, looking for another door. There wasn't one, but he caught Ava's eye through a window while Tilly busied herself pushing furniture against the cabin door. He held his finger to his lips. With Dave pounding on the door, Tilly didn't notice Ava cracking open the window. "Shh. Where's Mila?"

She pointed to a heap on the bed. "She's sleeping. I think Tilly drugged her. She'd never sleep through this."

"I'll be right back. Stay quiet."

Henry walked back to the front of the cabin and whispered to Emily. "You start pounding and talking. Dave and I will go in through the window."

Emily banged loudly and screamed, "You can't do this, Tilly. Think of the poor girls. How could you kill their mother?"

Finally, a response. "Poor mother? Do you know what Faith was doing to Mila?"

"What was she doing?" Emily screamed through the door, hoping to keep Tilly distracted.

"She was making her sick. For attention. I looked it up online. They call it Munchausen by Proxy. She made Mila sick to draw attention to herself."

"But Mila seemed well enough."

"She hadn't yet physically harmed Mila, but she was about to start. Seizures? I never witnessed one. Neither did Ava. Dairy intolerance? That girl chugs ice cream like the Good Humor man after fasting for Ramadan. She doesn't have a dairy allergy."

"Why didn't you report her if you suspected foul play?" asked Emily.

"I threatened to but she said no one would ever believe me. Especially after what happened to my daughter."

"Tilly, what happened to your daughter? I didn't know you had children."

"My ex-husband, my little Meredith's father. He was supposed to be watching her but he didn't. She ate a box of laundry pods. He didn't even notice. When I came to pick her up, she was already dead. I should have protected her. I should have stopped him. She was only three years old. I wasn't going to let the same thing happen to Mila."

"Faith wasn't hurting Mila, was she? Didn't she just pretend Mila had those seizures?"

"But she was about to cross the line. I found a bottle of Syrup of Ipecac in her room. Dave was planning to bring her back to court to fight for custody again. She was going to make Mila sick and say he did it."

"Dave wasn't here, though. How would that have worked?" asked Emily.

"He'd called and threatened to come up here to see the girls a few days before she died. That's when Faith agreed he could come and visit them for one afternoon. That's when she planned to make Mila sick and make sure Dave would never have a chance to be with the girls again."

"How do you know this?" asked Emily.

"She told me. She asked me to lie to the police and say Dave threatened to kill the girls if she didn't agree to share custody."

"So you killed Faith? Poisoned her cheesecake while it sat in the fridge?"

"Yes. Yes, I did."

At that moment, Emily heard furniture banging and the sound of Henry and Dave's voices. Tilly screamed. Henry burst the door open from the inside and let Emily in. Dave had Tilly in a choke hold.

"We got her," said Henry. "The girls are safe."

"I hear a siren. What took the police so long to get here?" said Dave.

Emily said, "Remember the truck accident? I'll bet they had trouble getting around it."

A few minutes later, Megan and Ron ran into the cabin. Ron secured the handcuffs while Megan read Tilly her rights.

Dave said, "Mila! Is she okay?' He went over to the bed and shook her. "Mila, Mila, are you okay?"

Mila moaned. "Daddy? Where are we?"

"We're safe, honey. Safe and sound."

Chapter 26

Emily woke up under her comforter, rolled over, and looked at her clock. 6 p.m. Henry slept beside her. The nap had done its job. When they got back from the cabin after rescuing the girls, she was sure she wouldn't be up to dinner at the inn tonight, but Maddy begged, and Emily couldn't say no. Henry stirred beside her.

"What time is it?" He pulled himself up on his elbows.

"6:00. We have to be at dinner in an hour."

"I wonder what this plan of Maddy's is? Do you have any idea?"

"No, but I think Coralee is in on it also. I'm going to jump in the shower."

"In a million years I wouldn't have guessed Tilly was the murderer."

"After what happened with her daughter, I can understand how the thought of Mila being harmed made her crazy and overprotective. She loves that little girl."

"She had other avenues of protecting Mila without murdering her mother. She could have called DCF, for example."

"Her daughter's tragic death derailed her. I understand. I'm to this day carrying around guilt over not protecting my sister. I'll never forgive myself. She never would have drowned if I'd been watching her like I was supposed to."

"You have to let that go. As much as you loved your sister, you can't bring her back."

Maddy knocked on the door. "Are you both up? Make sure you're ready to go on time."

"Yes, ma'am," Henry called through the door. "Emily, go take your shower so I have time to take one too."

"You could always join me. It'd save time."

"Save time...Yep, I'm in." He had his clothes off before she had the chance to turn on the water.

When they arrived at the Outside Inn, Coralee had portioned off an area by the windows overlooking the ice glazed golf course. With the glow from the full moon and the help of a few strategically placed torch lights, the lawn glistened like a frozen wonderland. Pat and Megan were already seated and sipping wine from the local winery.

Megan, dressed in a winter-white skirt and silk blouse, said, "We need this after the afternoon we had! Emily and Henry, the Sugarbury Falls police department says thank you once again for working with us to solve a murder." She raised her glass.

Maddy said, "Coralee made a special meal. Pasta alfredo with glazed pears."

Henry said, "That sounds a little weird, but I'll trust her culinary creativity."

Emily said, "I've never had anything here that didn't meet or exceed my expectations."

Henry cleared his throat. "You have to admit that the cauliflower brownies weren't really edible."

Coralee came to the table. "I heard that. I have cheesecake on tonight's dessert menu. Just kidding. It'll be a while before I make another cheesecake."

After dinner, Maddy and Pat excused themselves from the table.

"What are they up to?" asked Megan.

"I have no idea," said Emily. "I know it's something important. Maddy about blew a gasket when I said I might be too tired to eat out tonight."

Coralee reappeared. "You're wanted in the cat café. Follow me."

Henry whispered to Emily, "What the heck?"

"Just play along," said Emily. "I have a hunch."

Coralee opened the door to the cat café. Strings of twinkling lights sparkled across the ceiling. Candles glowed, filling the room with the scent of vanilla. Rose petals covered the floor.

Maddy played a simplified version of *The Wind Beneath my Wings* on her flute, then Pat, holding Tito, came into the room. He'd changed into a tux.

"Go ahead, Tito." Tito sprung from his arms. Maddy, standing behind Megan, called him over. Tito wore a sign around his neck.

Megan cried. "No way." She read the sign aloud. "You gato marry me."

"Well? What do you say," said Pat." Gato is Spanish for cat."

"I say 'Si! Si, si, si! Te amo.' I love you."

Tears streamed down her cheeks. Pat got down on one knee and pulled a diamond ring from his pocket. "Megan, I never thought I'd find love a second time around, but you make my life worth living." He slipped the ring on her finger. She hugged him and smothered him with kisses.

Megan wiped her eyes. "How did you think of such a clever idea?"

"It was Maddy's idea."

Henry said, "Good thing Tito didn't run away when you started play the flute, Maddy."

"Always the supportive father."

Emily said, "So do you have a date?"

Pat said, "I don't know. We'll have to discuss it. I do know where we're going for our honeymoon."

"Where?"

"Majorca. Spain. We'll fly into Barcelona and spend a few days there first."

Megan hugged him. "You know I've always dreamed of going to Spain."

"Yes, I know."

Emily couldn't stop the tears from flowing.

"Maddy, you're a gem," said Megan. "I'll never forget this. You will be a bridesmaid, right?"

"Wow, I'd love to. I've never been in a wedding before."

"And Emily? You'll be a bridesmaid, too I hope."

"I'd be honored."

Henry cleared his throat.

Pat said, "Well, buddy? You'll be my best man?"

"You bet. As long as I don't have to wear a frilly dress."

Coralee brought up a bottle of champagne. "I brought Maddy sparkling cider."

Pat said, "A toast to great friends, love, and new beginnings." Glasses clinked.

Megan said, "And to Tito. I've been talking about getting a pet. I can adopt him, right?"

Maddy said, "I can't think of a better engagement present."

Emily's phone vibrated. "Excuse me a minute." She stepped into the corridor. "Mom? I didn't know you were back from your cruise already."

"Emily, honey, I have some news. It's about your sister…"

THE END

ABOUT THE AUTHOR

 Diane Weiner is a veteran public school teacher and mother of four children. She has enjoyed reading for as long as she can remember. She has fond memories of reading Nancy Drew and Mary Higgins Clark on snowy weekend afternoons in upstate New York and yearned to write books that would bring that kind of enjoyment to her readers. Being an animal lover, she is a vegetarian and shares her home with two adorable cats. In her free time, she enjoys running, attending community theater productions, and spending time with her family (especially going to the mall with her teenage daughter and getting Dairy Queen afterwards).

The Tainted Course, is the fourth in Diane's Sugarbury Falls series. The first book in this series, *A Deadly Course,* recently received an Eric Hoffer International Book Competition Finalist Award for general fiction. The second is *Murder, of Course.* The third is *Clearing the Course.*

Diane also writes the Susan Wiles Schoolhouse mysteries.

Visit dianeweinerauthor.com to find out more about the author.

Made in the USA
Columbia, SC
20 December 2022

74469467R00124